A QUESTION OF INHERITANCE

A QUESTION OF INHERITANCE

A cot death – unexpected and shocking. Especially for the mother of the child, Mrs Florence Bennet, née Maisie Atkins, an actress past her prime who has provided her older husband with a much longed-for heir. A violent death twenty-two years on starts a police investigation which is set to begin a quest at home and abroad into the past to try and uncover the truth.

A Question Of Inheritance

by

Josephine Bell

Dales Large Print Books
Long Preston, North Yorkshire,
BD23 4ND, England.

British Library Cataloguing in Publication Data.

Bell, Josephine
    A question of inheritance.

    A catalogue record of this book is
    available from the British Library

    ISBN   1-84262-417-2 pbk

First published in Great Britain in 1980
by Hodder & Stoughton Ltd.

Copyright © 1980 by D.B. Ball

Cover illustration © Anthony Monaghan

The moral right of the author has been asserted

Published in Large Print 2005 by arrangement with
Curtis Brown

Dales Large Print is an imprint of Library Magna Books Ltd.

Printed and bound in Great Britain by
T.J. (International) Ltd., Cornwall, PL28 8RW

For

Graham Watson

In gratitude and affection, and because he
offered the basis of the plot

PART I

1953, Autumn

1

They sat in silence, staring before them, not at one another. Percy Bennet fixed his gaze on the fire, severe, unyielding, waiting for submission. Florence, his young wife, watched the rain streaming down the long window and beyond that in a slanting downpour on the lawn and on the tossing trees at the bottom of the lawn.

The weather, a miserable English autumn, supported her conclusion, unendurable, unbelievable, hopeless.

'I can't go on like this,' she said at last, in a dead voice. 'I don't know how you can ask me to.'

He answered at once, still patient, still waiting for the usual collapse; not unkind, but bored.

'I fail to understand the trouble. Mrs Somerton has always been an excellent housekeeper. The place gives you no trouble, or need not. With Gladys to clean, your sole job and responsibility is Philip–'

She interrupted him.

'It wasn't so bad until Nurse Barker left. She got him partly weaned for me. I know he isn't any trouble – sleeps most of the time

– in the garden when it isn't like today. But he's still only four months old. I don't know anything about babies. Mrs Somerton never talks to me about him. She hates me!'

'That is nonsense,' he said. 'Besides, what would she know about babies at her age? Her only child, if he's still alive, must be nearly twenty. Nurse Barker had finished the job she came for, so there was no point in keeping her on, was there?'

He stopped his reasonable arguments, for they had had the desired effect. Florence was crying now, the satisfactory broken sobs and little moans that always led to collapse into his welcoming arms, followed by a peace in which he reigned alone, but supreme as before.

Encouraging this consummation he said gently, 'You know how grateful I am for our little son. I think I have shown you how much I admire your achievement.'

Gratitude had been declared a few days ago with a really very pretty emerald and diamond brooch that had belonged to his mother. He had had the Edwardian setting lightened to make it appear modern, thinking she would appreciate that.

She had done so, was gratified for a present more valuable than any she had ever received. But she had not missed learning its provenance, for Mrs Somerton had not failed to explain it to her. So the brooch was part of Percy's endless miserliness, part of that entire self-concentration, that had been, she knew now, the sole motive for his wish to marry her.

She, an unsuccessful actress, a pretty girl without talent, but with a romantic love of the theatre, had found herself stranded on tour two years ago. After ten years of struggle, the face still pretty, but the heart no longer expectant, Percy Bennet had seen her, arranged to meet her, summed up her degree of anxiety, of danger; went on to win her as a wife.

In order to provide him with an heir. That had been his sole true motive. It speaks much for the intensity of his purpose that he did not find it too wasteful, too expensive, altogether too risky, in terms of personal sacrifice.

But no, he must have an heir. Garwood House had been in the family for over two hundred years. Before that the Bennet family had built their fortune upon ships, trading from Bristol, and when wealthy enough had settled in Dorset to continue trading from southern ports and had raised Garwood in a secluded valley, near the village of Broxbourne, about twenty miles from Bere Abbas and thirty from the sea.

Percy had been fifth in line from that time. The fortune had continued to prosper, until Percy's father, showing a more frivolous disposition than his own sons had done, took to the horses instead of the hounds and began, by gambling at the races, an alarming breakdown of that solid foundation. This was only halted when Percy took command. His drastic measures became a habit as he grew older. Conservation turned into deprivation. Until he found himself without friends, without wife or child, without a living relative except a brother-in-law and sister in Canada, with an ancient dwelling in grave need of repair, and carefully preserved invested wealth, the management of which gave him regular work of a kind, but no pleasure, only a dreary, smug sort of satisfaction.

Florence was thirty-two when Philip was born. Percy had shown her so much consideration and thoughtful care during the pregnancy that she imagined he did at last love her: whereas, as she now understood him, his warmth of feeling was for the child alone. But she was grateful none the less for the extra help in the house; here, Gladys, her personal little maid, apart from the dailies Mrs Somerton engaged and directed, was still at Garwood when she came back from the hospital maternity ward.

Her delivery had been perfectly normal, quite a routine job, the midwife told her, and she had a normal, healthy little boy. Nothing startling for the records; nothing for Mr Bennet to make such a song and

14

dance over. You'd think no man over fifty had ever had a first child before, especially with a strong young woman like herself, barely the wrong side of thirty.

Florence discounted this rather snide summing-up and was delighted to find a fully trained nursery nurse waiting in the hall of the hospital when she arrived there with Philip in her arms. Percy was waiting outside in the car.

With an heir in the house, she fondly imagined, his father would continue to mellow, to unbend, to become a human, caring head of family, promoter of happiness. Characteristically Percy had put off doing up any of the old nursery quarters of the house. She had not pressed him to do so because these old rooms, much dilapidated, were too remote, too dark with their small barred windows, too damp and cold for any modern use. But there must be somewhere, on the first floor preferably, where Philip could begin to assemble his toys, his books, have his meals, learn to walk, to play, when the garden was too cold or too wet.

Arriving back at Garwood from the hospital with Philip still held in her arms, Percy beside her and Nurse Barker sitting on the passenger seat beside Grant, the chauffeur, Florence found to her delight that the very room she had picked out but never had courage to propose, was precisely that to which Percy now led her.

She was too surprised, too grateful, to do more than stare about her. It was a perfect nursery, wallpaper, paint, small furniture, comfortable table and chair, safe heating and lighting and a budgerigar in a cage.

'Oh, darling!' Florence cried with a catch in her voice, 'You are wonderful!'

Nurse Barker found this an admirable cue for action. She took the baby from her young, emotional mistress, and watched Mr Bennet, clearly at the peak of well-earned success, lead her away.

Four months later, driven by cold, discomfort, anxiety, loneliness and a prickling sense of injustice, sitting unwillingly beside a sullen fire, Florence returned her gaze from the streaming misery of the rain-soaked garden to the stony face of her husband. He expected her to give in as usual. This time she would not give in. And she had the child. She would use the child. She straightened herself and spoke sharply.

'You sent Nurse Barker away too soon. She was showing me how to manage Philip. I was completely ignorant about babies. You knew that. I was never at home – always on tour. It worries me all the time, whether I'm doing his food properly. Gladys helps, but now if she has to work in the house for Mrs Somerton–'

'Mrs Somerton has given me her notice,'

16

Percy said coldly, his eyes fixed on his wife. 'I have accepted it and I have engaged another housekeeper. She will engage a housemaid of her own choice and will do all the cooking herself.'

'You never told me! None of it! It's – it's outrageous!'

'I would have told you quietly this evening,' he said. 'I did not want to upset you before time.'

This was too much.

'Before I could object! Before I could do anything to persuade Mrs Somerton to stay. Before I could decide how–'

'It is *I* who decide matters in this house.' His voice was thick with anger now. It drove her beyond prudence, beyond foresight.

'Yes, *you* decide! Everything – always! Not any longer, Percy. This goes too far. I shall leave you! Philip goes with me! If you try to stop us I'll take you to court. They'll give me custody, not you, selfish, self-centred, miserly pig that you are!'

She was on her feet, inwardly terrified of what she was threatening, but consciously putting on one of those third-rate Victorian dramas of dreary domestic upheaval that had provided her bread and butter on the stage.

'You forget yourself,' Percy told her, correctly but without intention playing his part of the cruel husband. 'You have no means of

17

carrying out such a threat and you know it. As for my son–'

'Yes, poor lamb. But he's my son, too.'

Percy rose from his chair and moved to the door. But he turned before he opened it and said, with the same maddening, cold, vicious calm, 'Need I remind you that you have no means to carry out this stupid, vulgar threat? Nor will you ever have that independence. Philip is my heir: all that I have will be his when I die. If that should happen before he comes of age I have appointed a guardian to administer his estate and to provide you with an allowance during your lifetime. But you will have no power over his upbringing now or in the future, at any time. I hope you understand that and will remember it.'

He turned back to the door, hesitated a second, but went out, shutting it behind him.

Florence soon left the room herself, to go upstairs to the nursery, for it was nearly six o'clock, when Philip's next feed was due.

With Gladys to help her she carried out the routine she had been taught by Nurse Barker. She was fond of her funny little baby, with his mop of soft black hair that was already wearing off the back of his head; that big wobbly head, the straight solid little body, tiny legs, arms already swelling into use, the searching, clutching small hands.

18

All strange, astonishing to one as ignorant of children as herself.

She was still nervous as she handled him. She had far less confidence than Gladys and now, this evening, was repelled by Percy's cruel ultimatum and all that it implied.

Supposing she left, alone, without further notice. Gladys would hold the fort until Nurse Barker or another of her sort came to the rescue. Philip was too young to mind the change, would be better off, probably, without her.

But she found him whimpering, waiting for his meal, impatient of Gladys's efforts to curb his cries. And when she took him into her own arms and sat, spooning the semi-solid pap into the eager little mouth before giving him the more familiar bottle to finish with, she knew the wave of tenderness she felt was true and natural and most desirable. If she left, Philip must go with her. But how could she leave? Was she not utterly helpless?

The prospect that night was anything but hopeful. Percy appeared at the dinner table, but went to his study immediately after an uncomfortable, mainly silent meal. She sat alone, tried to read, but finding it impossible, wrote a long, rather confused letter about Philip, about her difficulties with Percy, about that evening's quarrel, to an old friend of her acting days, Amy Tupper, who was much older than she was and had soon given up the stage, except in an amateur capacity, to help with local dramatics and other good works. Old Amy might advise her how to live without money, how to earn a living for herself and child, without talent, without skill, without patronage.

When she went to bed she gave Philip his last feed of the day and settled him in his cot in her room. Percy had slept in the dressing room adjoining, since she came back from the hospital. As a rule he expected her to go to him to say goodnight, though he never visited her in turn and had made no advance beyond a few decidedly cool kisses. This night she found the connecting door locked.

How like him! How essentially childish! Her sense of injustice went beyond anger, beyond self-pity, to a kind of shame that an ageing man who was her husband and the father of her child, could so demean himself.

The next morning, however, found the situation restored to something less like a Victorian melodrama, more like the home of a modern, prosperous man of business. To begin with there was a letter from Percy, brought to her in bed by Gladys, with the usual cup of coffee. Percy had decided that she was 'run down' and in need of a change, which would also benefit Philip. So he had arranged by telephone to his London office that a room would be taken for her at a Bournemouth guest house for convalescents and nursing mothers, for two weeks from the day after tomorrow. This would give her twenty-four hours to pack and arrange transport. He enclosed a cheque which she could change into the necessary cash as she needed it. The guest house would be paid for in advance. He was going to London himself that morning and hoped to find her restored to her usual co-operative, cheerful self when she came back from Bournemouth. He had not lost his past regard for her and the happiness she had given him and was her loving husband, Percy.

Astonished, Florence got up at once and hurried downstairs, but Percy had already left the house. In the kitchen Gladys was alone, drinking tea and eating cornflakes for her breakfast. Mrs Somerton was not there.

'She says she's off,' Gladys said, shaking her head in disapproval.

'What d'you mean?'

'Give 'er notice. Not staying now master's gone.'

'But she can't do that!' Florence was indignant.

'Who says I can't?'

Mrs Somerton stood in the doorway, red-faced and trembling.

'Oh, there you are!' Florence tried to keep

21

her voice low and steady. 'I understood from Mr Bennet that you had given notice, a month's notice, and I was very sorry to hear it, when you've been here so long.'

Her effort was unrewarded. It seemed to have the opposite effect to what she intended. Mrs Somerton's face grew an even deeper red, she clenched her hands and stepped forward so threateningly that Florence retreated behind Gladys's chair. The girl seemed unmoved however, just finished her cornflakes and her tea and stood up, wiping her mouth on the back of her hand.

'Boiled egg, as usual, Mrs Bennet?' she asked, quietly.

Florence, whose only wish was to escape from the kitchen, murmured, 'Yes, please, Gladys,' and made for the door. But as she reached it she heard Mrs Somerton's strident voice in attack.

'Yes, after all these years! Slaving for him and no one else putting up with his mean ways and the saving and scraping and complaints of extravagance. And him a young man, too, in his thirties coming into the estate, sole heir, he was. You'll look after me now Mother's gone, won't you, Sommie? he says.'

Florence turned. The Bennet saga – here it was, demanding a hearing at least, in common decency.

Mrs Somerton acknowledged the gesture:

it stopped the flow of her recital but it did not soften its rage, only brought it to an abrupt end.

'I understand you will be going on a holiday, madam,' she said, polite now but reluctant. 'So there will be no point in my remaining. The new housekeeper is due to come in a day or two. I shall pack and leave this afternoon. My nephew is going to pick me up with my things in his van. The other dailies were discharged yesterday.'

Florence nodded. Percy had told her this, last night: she had not taken it in, not all of it. Too much occupied with their battle of wills.

'Gladys here will see you off tomorrow, won't you, Gladys?'

The girl nodded, not answering. But later on that day, when she was helping Florence to pack a second suitcase with Philip's clothes, she said in a worried voice, 'You'll be all alone in the house tonight, Mrs Bennet. I'd offer to sleep in, but my mum would create if I did. She's scared to be alone herself and dad's on night shift this week.'

'That's all right,' Florence told her. 'I don't mind a bit. I've got Philip.'

She laughed, but Gladys gave her a queer look, meaning she hardly thought it a laughing matter.

How desperately, horribly true that was Florence discovered at ten o'clock, when she went up to give the baby his last feed and settle him in his cot in her room.

He had been very quiet all the afternoon, but had seemed contented, if not lively, at six and had gone to sleep again without any preliminary crying soon after that, while she moved about the nursery tidying away everything she was not going to take with her to Bournemouth. The guest house was able to provide small bath tubs, but mothers were expected to bring their children in carry-cots; if possible the sort with stands and frames that converted them into standing cots and also into prams. These fittings she had already put into the boot of her own small car, so as not to forget to take them with her.

When she went upstairs at ten she was feeling calm and competent. She had paid Percy's cheque into her own account that morning and had drawn it all out again, partly in cash, chiefly in travellers' cheques. She meant to get up early and had warned Gladys of this intention, telling the girl not to bother with the early cup of coffee in her room, but to make the breakfast pot and boil her an egg.

Before going to her bath she looked into Philip's cot. Fast asleep still, she decided. Good little fellow. Really, he was no trouble. His little hand was clenched round his favourite toy, the bone ring Gladys had given him – a teething ring, with three little bells on it that tinkled as he waved it about.

She had a good soak, indulging herself in Percy's absence, for he grew impatient if she stayed too long away from him, after he was in bed himself. Or had done until the routine was altered by Philip's arrival. The routine was going to be altered in other ways now, she promised herself. This holiday was a forerunner.

But when, the warmed milk on her bed-table, she stooped to lift the child, instant fear swept over her. For the tiny hand and arm, instead of stiffening, clutching, hung limply: the big head fell back, unnaturally far back, before she caught it to bring it forward, when it rolled horribly from side to side, while she screamed in panic and began to shake and pat and rub that strong, solid little body, now a poor limp shell, a lifeless corpse.

For Philip was terrifyingly, inexplicably, disastrously, dead.

2

Florence collapsed, fainting, on the floor beside the cot. Before that she had laid the small limp body down with more tenderness than she had ever shown before to Percy's son. For Philip had not been a love child, he had not been the child of a true marriage, but of a coldly engineered bargain. She had secured an established home, less comfortable, far less luxurious, than she had expected. In return she had conceived and nourished Percy's heir, had brought him forth with far less suffering than her friends had prophesied for her and this, in her opinion, had completed her side of the contract. Percy had reneged on the sequel, he expected a further bargain for the care and happiness of wife and child, in the production, expected of course, of a companion for Philip, together with suitable staff, which he could well afford, to look after them all.

When the shock and distress of her discovery had begun to wear off, Florence went over these thoughts with increased bitterness, mingled now with panic. Philip had gone, slipped away from life without warning, without apparent pain, without any kind of struggle. There was a name for it. Cot death. She had always thought this was an excuse for some kind of neglect or stupidity or even a wish to be relieved of an unwanted burden by some subtle means unknown to doctors or the Law.

But no, it was real. Philip had been very well all his tiny life. She had not been able to feed him herself, but that was not unusual, he had thrived, seemingly, until this very evening.

As she recovered her senses Florence struggled to her feet. Panic displaced the shock. It couldn't be true – the doctor – she must call the doctor. What could she say? That the baby was dead! Just like that, dead! He wouldn't believe her!

She looked at Philip again. Oh yes, he was dead. No breath, no little rapid heart beat, and, when she carried him to the bedside table lamp, a strange, sad, bluish-yellow pallor had spread over the little features. Death having struck, was proceeding on his course of dissolution.

Her panic grew. Her only wish, her sole intention now, was to escape from this house, this life, this appalling responsibility. Ring Percy? Lay it all on her husband? Her useless, cold-hearted, miserly husband? If she called the doctor, who could do nothing, he would call Percy. She might as well kill herself. Florence Bennet might as well die with her baby.

But her other self, Maisie Atkins, struggling actress, said aloud, 'Don't be such a bloody damned fool! Go, yes. You ought never to have mixed yourself up with this fairy tale. Get out, *now*, and get out at once!'

Once decided, she worked quickly and as always, with no thought but for herself. She looked out her passports, the one in the name of Maisie Atkins, valid for another year, she was thankful to find, and the new one in her married name, with Philip on it as well. She had taken this out for her honeymoon with Percy in France and had added the baby to it when she expected Percy to take them both abroad during the coming summer.

She would go before Gladys arrived in the morning. She ought to leave the girl a note of explanation, but then decided this would be a mistake. Gladys knew where she was supposed to be going and would not worry. The new housekeeper did not expect to see her until her fortnight in Bournemouth was over. No doubt Percy had notified the woman of his own return. So no questions were likely to be asked until she had had time, as Miss Atkins, to disappear on the Continent, if possible finding work. But anyway, for good.

And Philip? Poor sad little corpse, so crudely, deliberately designed to fill two

29

selfish people's desires for the enjoyment of property; so mysteriously withdrawn from life. Garwood had been preserved for three hundred years and in her opinion was not worth the tragic care that had been given it, not only in this last sordid transaction, but in other, earlier efforts and agonies.

In grief, in fear, in a sort of distraction with her essential helplessness, Florence decided that Philip must stay at Garwood. Whatever possible danger it might place her in, she would give him a decent burial. She could not try any other kind of disposal; she shuddered away from fire. There was no water, no lake or pond or stream in the garden or in the fields near by. She was not a countrywoman and did not consider the danger to any shallow grave from prowling animals or inquisitive human beings.

But she had the sense to choose a spot, in the middle of a thick shrubbery, where she would not have to cut turf and where the surface already had a layer of fallen leaves and twigs, easily replaced. Also she found at the back of the garage an old rusted tin box large enough for her purpose and which she felt impelled to turn into a coffin worthy of her little son. She lined it with a silk petticoat, nearly new, laid Philip upon it and wrapped him in a soft wool blanket she had knitted for him herself. She pulled the damaged lid of the box down and fastened it with a piece of artificial string she found in a drawer in the kitchen. Then she carried it out to the grave. The rain had stopped some time before, but the trees dripped.

It took her longer than she expected to finish the work of burial. The hole needed was far deeper than she had first imagined. Six inches below the surface there were roots everywhere, most of them strong, many impossible to cut through with a spade. The night was very dark when she began the work, for which she was thankful. Before she had done, had sunk Philip deep enough, added a few stones to the battered top of the tin coffin and covered all with a thick layer of earth and leaves, she found a rake and worked at the surrounding surface to make it look all alike, as far as she could judge.

By that time she had grown accustomed to the night. She understood for the first time in her life that no night was really dark, in the way a lighted room, with curtains or shutters closed, could be dark, or a passage between houses. She had begun to see shapes of the garden and particularly of the bushes among which Philip now lay.

There were shapes and also there were sounds. A hunting owl flew about the garden, perhaps curious about her presence; there were small squeaks; agitated rustlings, perhaps a response to the owl's arrival. Humans today might sleep easily, she thought; once, long ago, lying out in wild thickets, with wolves as well as owls, they had been afraid, threatened too.

She cried then, partly for her lost child, but chiefly for herself, for the vast complexity of the next moves and how to make them safely, until she would at last be free to begin her life all over again.

Dawn found Florence on the outskirts of Weymouth, drawn into the side of the road, considering how best she might dispose of the car.

Her main intention was to park it at a garage, ostensibly for a fortnight's trip to France. She would pay in advance and they would do what they liked with it when she never turned up to claim it. She had been through all the pockets very carefully, removing maps and guides and all those odd scraps of paper, notes and bills and crumpled ageing directions about journeys of years ago. Most of them she now threw into the thick grass and bushes at the wayside. Only the more recent, more useful maps she left to look like the normal furniture of a woman's car.

Locked away in the boot were Philip's small carry-cot and the folding frame with wheels that turned it into a pram. As she had fitted these parts into the boot, covering them with a picnic ground sheet and rug, she remembered Percy's approval when she bought the outfit during the last month of her pregnancy. Well, it was cheap enough, as post-war prices went and the implication must be that the reason for her stinginess, her meanness matching his, must be that neither looked forward to a long use for such things. There would be no large family. At most one more, to keep Philip company.

With the boot full, Florence had put her two suitcases on the back seat, together with her mackintosh belted round one of them and her umbrella fastened to the other. She checked all of her luggage, consulted a guide of Britain's sea coast that had an enlarged map of Weymouth, turned up her headlights and drove on.

It was after six but still, in November with a heavy clouded sky, quite dark from a driver's point of view. However, when she came to outlying houses and countrified pavements there were occasional street lamps too at corners and she had no difficulty in reading street signposts and the names of the roads. When she judged she was near enough to the port, she looked out for an all-night garage and came to one where a couple of lorries were parked with their drivers stretching their legs and arms beside their cabs, and yawning widely.

The pumps were manned by a sleepy boy, who was quite incapable of understanding what she wanted. Besides, it was not the kind of place she wanted, so rather against her wish to appear in any way unusual, she appealed to the lorry drivers for advice.

'Car park? Long term?' They looked at one another and shook their heads.

'No, miss. Not in our line. Town park's central. You can't miss it.'

'Somewhere to leave the car, I mean. While I go abroad – on business,' she added, feeling the withdrawal from, and envy of, one who went abroad at will and alone, instead of properly booked for a holiday in Spain.

'You want the airfield, then? They have parking.'

'It doesn't matter,' Florence said, beginning to panic again.

But the boy, who had by now filled the lorries' tanks, came round to her side of the car.

'You sailing, miss?' he asked.

'Yes.' Clearly he was not as gormless as he looked. 'And I want to lay up the car for two weeks.'

'First on the right here and left at the lights and it's on the left. They open at six. Try there.'

'Thanks a lot.'

She fumbled in her bag for a suitable tip, but the boy was gone by the time she looked up again so she switched on and left, hoping she had not made much impression by her enquiry.

The boy was right. It was just before seven when she came to another lighted garage and here there were two men, one in overalls, one in a dark suit about to discard his jacket.

He shrugged it back over his shoulders when she got out of the car, but turned away into his office. Florence followed him and explained what she wanted.

She explained that she would be away for two weeks, travelling for her theatrical group in France and Italy. She showed him her passport, Maisie Atkins, actress, with a perfectly recognisable photograph. As she turned away from the man, feeling in her bag for the passport, she saw that she was still wearing her wedding ring. Slipping it off was easy, leaving it in the bag as she presented the passport.

'I would like to pay the rent in advance,' she said, firmly.

'I wouldn't put the car up otherwise, Miss Atkins,' he said. There was no emphasis on the name as he spoke it, but she could not help wondering if he had seen the ring when she first went up to him beside the petrol pumps.

He named a price, a steep one, which she paid, saying as she took the receipt, 'And now can you call me a taxi to take me and my bags to the ship. I want to go by sea to St Malo.'

He looked surprised, then glanced at the clock.

'Got your ticket?'

'No.'

'You've not got much time.'

'Oh dear.'

She suddenly felt weak, helpless, afraid. What must she do to get away? Southampton? Everywhere she was leaving tracks, doing strange things, drawing attention to herself.

'Tell you what,' the man said. 'I'll drive with you to the office at the quay, you get your ticket and take your bags on board and I'll bring the car back here. Right?'

'Thank you very much,' Florence said, with real gratitude.

They drove off at once, the man at the wheel. He drove very fast but well, and in a very few minutes set her down at the office where she secured a single ticket to St Malo and learned that she had five minutes to get aboard before the gangways would be taken in.

The man took the bags, they hurried along; Florence was urged up the gangway, her bags were almost thrown after her. Bells rang, voices yelled, passengers on either side of her, behind her, pushing in front of her, waved and shouted and screamed to those who were seeing them off.

Florence shouted and waved with them. She tried to see the man on the quay, but he seemed to have gone. As they slid out of the narrow harbour she could see the dark line of the coast on the other side of the bay and a little later the flashing beam of the light vessel at its wide mouth, with the tall Portland Bill tower sweeping its great arc far out across the Channel.

It was only after Florence had found herself a seat below, with her two bags beside her, and had secured coffee and sandwiches, that she began to wonder why that garage proprietor had treated her so kindly, accepting her account of herself without real question, helping her so efficiently to catch the packet. Was he going to nick the car? Well, he was welcome to it. Or was he just honest, had he seen her ring and was amused by her obvious escape from a husband. If so, how flattering! Percy had almost made her feel her looks were gone as well as her charm and everything she had always taken for granted as her right and due from men. It had never moved Percy, when she showed distress or helpless fear. With this man – she didn't even know his name – it had worked instantly. Bless him, she almost hoped he *would* snitch the car before Percy got the powers that be on to finding it for him.

From St Malo she had no difficulty in finding a train for Paris. Her French, she discovered, with relief, had survived the last few years without practice, so it was easy and familiar to meet the various officials at the port, the customs hall, the railway station. She dared not stop in Paris, but merely crossed the city, found herself another snack and by late afternoon was on her way south.

Arrived in Marseilles she already had a plan for her next move. About six years ago she had been engaged by a theatrical touring company to visit a number of Italian cities where there were universities likely to appreciate Shakespeare in English, softened by two modern English comedies. The enterprise had been conceived by academics of the two countries. Passing into commercial hands, it had been totally unsuccessful. So much so that after several very unnerving failures in the industrial north, with Milan the most humiliating, Florence had found herself finally abandoned in Naples, from where, with three other members of the company, and less than half the wages due to them, they had found a local coaster willing to convey them by sea to Marseilles.

Florence had remembered this sad story and the outcome as her train sped to the south from Paris. She knew where she had landed in Marseilles, part of that busy port far from tourists and yet respectable enough not to draw attention to a quiet youngish Englishwoman travelling as cheaply as possible. The typical British spinster schoolmarm, she thought wryly, but again unremarkable, as far as the authorities were concerned. And Naples had one great advantage. There was a kind, fat, Neapolitan landlady, accustomed to lodgers, theatrical, artistic, or student, all hard-up, but solvent. Eleanora always made sure of that.

Florence was fortunate again. She began to feel that once away from Garwood House and its deadly, lowering atmosphere, the world was perhaps a better place than she had grown to expect. She had no trouble finding a suitable craft and paid for her single passage at a rate only slightly higher than she had hoped. She spent the voyage for the most part sleeping away the shock, the loss, and the bitter agitation of the total collapse of her marriage.

When she disembarked, among a handful of other passengers, mostly men, middle-aged, drab, commercial, she handled her two suitcases with strength renewed, warding off a swarm of ragged would-be porters, who tried to snatch them from her. Customs again, untidy, casual, bored, were a little roused by reading her profession, but decided, rightly, that she was no celebrity, and did not bother to open her second bag, the one with Philip's clothes in it. In this they showed less interest than the French, to whom she had explained the little garments were for a friend who had recently given birth. She was believed, she hoped, though there was the routine search for drugs. With luck she had been forgotten in St Malo. Now in Naples only her own bag had been opened.

She blessed her luck, guardian angel or whatever, for holding once again, when she arrived at the well-remembered address. Eleanora was there, fatter than ever, no less kind and welcoming.

'Maisee! It is Maisee!' she cried with a following effusion in rapid Italian.

'Oui, c'est moi! Si, I mean,' Florence answered, stumbling between French and English in her effort to remember a few crumbs of Italian.

But Eleanora only laughed and screamed her joy in their reunion and Florence hugged her hostess and wept on her shoulder.

3

A long night's sleep, followed and preceded by a couple of ample meals, restored Florence to her normal health and energy. Her adult life had never been easy: whenever the future had promised well, as when Percy had taken a fancy for her, in the end he had proved to be a mean bastard, a miser, a louse. Her baby, carried so easily, born without fuss, danger, and far less pain than everyone had foretold, had vanished, poor little chap, as quietly, as undramatically, as he had arrived.

She had got over the shock now, she told herself. She hoped she had avoided any kind of aftermath, any punishment for suppressing all news, all possible discovery, of his death. She hoped she had escaped completely from her ill-advised marriage. She was Maisie Atkins for good now, or so she intended. But deep in herself she doubted her complete success. Real luck never came her way.

Nevertheless, Florence behaved with unexpected cheerfulness and good humour when she met Eleanora at noon on her second day in Naples. Her landlady congratulated her in her fluent, heavily accented American English, learned from contact with several of her emigrant relations, back on holiday to their native land.

'Now you look yourself again, honey,' she said. 'So ill, so white, so *old*, my poor Maisie! Some guy do you dirt? All alone? No job?'

'That's just it, Nora,' Florence said, putting an arm across Eleanora's wide shoulders. 'No jobs, and I need one badly. I've been round to the agents we had here three years ago, but they've gone. Packed it in, I suppose?'

'Vidal's?' Eleanora was scornful. 'Went off with the office furniture and the office typist and left a wad of debts high lika, lika Monte Cassino.'

'Where can I try, then?'

Eleanora had two names to offer but did not think much of either. In fact she suggested that Naples was not the best place to try for anything theatrical. The tourists got television in their hotels, they didn't want Italian theatre, certainly not the English kind, neither classical nor variety. They were not the kind that went to theatres at home.

Florence knew all this only too well. But she had to try harder before she decided to move on. Her money would not last for ever. If she could not find anything in the entertainment world she must try for something secretarial. Her Italian, always very patchy, had already begun to come back to her a little. Travel agencies, shipping firms, even municipal offices, might need an interpreter.

It was in Luccini's travel bureau that she met the woman with the baby. The woman seemed to be about her own age, much the same dark hair and eyes, but with a drawn anxious look in a face more lined and work-worn than Florence's had ever been, and with a complexion brown enough to have belonged to the northern shores of Africa rather than the south of Italy.

Florence felt drawn to this woman because she pitied her and because she guessed that the cause of her troubled expression might be on account of the child she held close in her arms.

It was a young baby, about Philip's age, she thought, with an unexpected pang of regret for her own loss. She moved nearer, took a seat in the row of chairs provided for would-be enquirers, of whom there was a surprising number. She smiled at the little face, staring at her over the mother's shoulder and was pleased, ridiculously so, she thought, when the mouth widened into a grin, showing toothless gums and spilling a warm dribble over the mother's back.

The latter exclaimed, pulled the baby

down roughly, making it cry, dabbed a dirty handkerchief at the wet spot, scolding with ever-diminishing vigour that ended with a resounding kiss to end the infant's hurt surprise.

'I'm afraid it was my fault,' Florence apologised in her halting Italian. 'I smiled at him because he is such a pretty child and he was gracious enough to smile back.'

'He is a little fool,' the mother said. 'He follows every lead. That is why – that is how–' She broke off abruptly, for her turn had come. In response to the invitation she gathered up the child, together with a large shopping bag, and moved to a distant table where a young man was waiting to attend to her wants and advise her.

Florence's enquiry took less time, for there was no vacancy for a foreigner on the staff, nor likely to be one. They had already engaged the extra hands for the next spring and summer seasons. She saw as she moved away that the woman with the baby was talking volubly. She wondered as she left the place what could such a person really want from a travel agency. But she put the question from her as she consulted Eleanora's list before walking on to the next name upon it.

She had no greater success. Her Italian was not good enough to ensure her any position as an interpreter. In fact she was greeted with ironic amusement, if not downright rudeness. She went back to her lodgings thoroughly discouraged. In fact so much so that she soon gave up the search for that day and instead walked first and then sat where she could enjoy the sea, with the long sweep of the bay in each direction, a misty view of Capri straight ahead and behind, to the south of the city, the plumed height of Vesuvius. She watched idly as hydrofoils set off from the harbour near by, rocking clumsily until they rose on their skids and drove away at speed, almost hidden by the spray they created. Beautiful scene! Beautiful pleasures! But not for her. Never for her.

The next day Florence was again walking beside the sea, wishing there was a proper beach with chairs and huts from which she could sunbathe and perhaps swim. She had been walking on the hill behind the shore, where on a road above the houses she found the upper branches of orange and lemon trees heavy with fruit, their trunks standing against the hill from the gardens of houses, whose roofs too she could look down upon. Some of these were having attention to their tiles from workmen using tree-trunks roughly trimmed, bound together with ropes, as scaffolding. She imagined the horror of British builders if they were asked to use such dangerous props. But these short, dark men seemed happy enough, certainly they showed no dissatisfaction with the job or its conditions.

So Florence, full of amused enjoyment of her surroundings, the sunshine, the late, ripe, unpicked fruit, the quiet sea sparkling and chuckling against the stones of the off-shore breakwaters, was in a generous mood of renewed confidence when she came across the woman with the baby, sitting with the child near a shore-side restaurant.

She went up to her and because there was an empty seat beside her sat down on it and said, 'Good morning.'

As the woman looked astonished, Florence went on.

'You were in that travel agency yesterday. Luccini's bureau, isn't it called? We spoke a few words.'

'I remember you now,' the woman answered. 'Yes, Luccini's. I heard you ask for employment.'

'You *heard?*'

'I was told. After you left. They did not understand why you should want to work as an interpreter or secretary.'

'Because my Italian is not good enough. But I understand everything you say now. We are speaking Italian now. Before we spoke English only, and your English is not very good, is it? Perhaps just American?'

They both laughed. But Florence's curiosity had been roused. She wanted to know

46

why this friendly person had learned the whole content of her interview with a man at Luccini's who seemed to be some sort of manager there.

'I will tell you,' the woman said. Her face had changed. It held again that expression of strain, of anxiety, even of dread, that had so surprised and worried Florence in their first encounter.

'I am a member of that family,' she explained. 'I am Paula Luccini. My husband is the Great Luccini himself, Federico.' As Florence showed no recognition of the name nor the reason of its fame, Paula drew herself up to explain with great dignity. 'His grandfather founded the troupe. Acrobats. Trapeze artistes. High-wire. Known over all the world. No circus is complete without Luccini.'

'Of course.' Florence was quick to excuse herself. 'I am, I was, an actress myself. I never had much time or opportunity to go to circuses. I was an only child, my parents – my father died too young–'

She stopped, astonished at herself for pouring out this garbled, half untrue, history of her life. Maisie Atkins's history. So unlike Florence's, so very unlike Mrs Bennet's. She pulled herself together.

'But the travel agency and the rest of the bureau? Did your husband set that up, too? Or is there a partnership? Forgive me, perhaps I should not ask?'

'Why not? I have already told you that I was curious to know your reason for going to the bureau. You took notice of my little Filippo. Why should you not be curious?'

'Then may I go on to ask you what very urgent business you yourself had at the bureau? You were called to one of the desks before I had my turn and you were still there when I left?'

To Florence's astonishment Signora Luccini covered her face with her hands and burst into loud sobs, rocking herself backwards and forwards in an extremity of anguish.

Naturally the baby who had seemed to be very fast asleep in his little push-chair when Florence sat down, now must have been roused by the uncontrolled sound of his mother's distress, in spite of the continuing background of lively city noise, for his thin, high wail was added to the turmoil. Heads of passers-by turned in their direction as the signora continued to rock herself to and fro and moan, while her little Filippo, expecting instant succour and failing to get it, raised his grief to anger and screamed in broken gasps as only a very young baby can.

Florence felt like running away, but she was afraid to do so. Too many people were staring, too many would see her as a foreigner, a potential enemy, a criminal perhaps. So she snatched up the child to stop that source of embarrassment at least.

To her surprise he stopped screaming at once, his breathing became normal, though occasionally disturbed by violent hiccups. Florence felt safe enough in his regard to reach a hand to the mother and pat her shoulder.

'You have frightened Filippo,' she said. 'But I have told him you are not really ill. Or are you?'

Signora Luccini recovered at once. The sobs were replaced by gasps of astonishment as she lifted her head to see her child smiling up at Florence and making those small burbling sounds that mimic speech in the very young. For several minutes she wiped her eyes, blew her nose, straightened her hair with clumsy hands, pulled down her skirt and jacket. Then she held out her arms for Filippo and took him on to her own lap. He seemed to be unmoved by the transfer.

'I will now go home,' she said. 'I make my apologies for this behaviour.'

'But why were you so upset? Was it my fault? What did I say – or do?'

Florence was unwilling to see her go, for she guessed the woman would be careful not to meet her again and she had begun to feel that with her and her wealthy successful business connections she might find herself some sort of employment, to keep her in Italy and hidden from any kind of search Percy must by now be starting to make.

For he must surely know that she had not arrived to take up her place with Philip at the private guest house in Bournemouth. That she had, in fact, with car, child, baggage for the two of them and the money in the form of travellers' cheques and cash, disappeared, leaving no trace of any kind. All this persuaded her to develop the new acquaintanceship. She, too, was shaken by her encounter with the baby. Another Philip. Extraordinary coincidence. Frightening, in a way.

Signora Luccini remained sitting, with Filippo again dozing on her lap. Florence spoke again, very gently, very slowly, in English now.

'It was not business of any kind that took you to the bureau, I think. Or it was family business, perhaps? It is no business of mine to ask you about it, unless of course, I can be of any help.'

She waited, while her companion's face gradually softened from its expression of distorted grief into one of hopelessness. Then, with her eyes fixed on the little sleeping face of her baby, she said, 'I told you my husband is the great head of the troupe. He is the high-wire man, no net, you understand. They have too much pride. Besides, the audience expect it. They hope for a fall: that is the supreme thrill.'

'Oh surely!' Florence was shocked, but she knew it was true. Man was born savage and cruel. These southern people were not hypocrites like the English, or some of the English.

'Oh, but yes. And he knows the troupe is less spectacular than it used to be. His father fell and was killed, from the trapeze, so two of his brothers made the bureau for holiday travel as well as circus tours. They learned to perform in childhood as all Luccini boys are taught, but they were afraid as they grew older.'

'But you are young, your husband cannot be very old now?'

'He is thirty-one. I am twenty-nine. I have three girls. They will dance well, but they have no talent for balance. It is Filippo here who will walk on the high-wire. My husband swears it. So he will be trained and I am afraid. So much afraid. He will perhaps fall as his grandfather fell and two older cousins and perhaps the great Federico himself. It is a madness in the blood. I am afraid.'

She was rocking herself to and fro as she finished speaking, but the tears were exhausted and the sobs silenced.

Florence understood the causes of her fear, but she did not feel the agitation. Surely Paula was worried far too soon. It would be years before any real decision had to be made. Even then the boy might have no talent, no aptitude for this sort of physical skill. He might not even like doing it, might decide for himself to follow some other bent and make a career for himself in quite a different direction. Since the end of the war children, especially those evacuated from towns to the country, had become very independent. But that was in England. In Italy the war had been different; invaded, fought over, after suffering or enjoying Mussolini's dictatorship. This topline acrobat, Federico Luccini, must have fought in the war until Mussolini collapsed. Better, perhaps, not to refer to that.

So she sat still, offering as much silent support and sympathy as she was capable of producing. This unusual contact and the most unusual problem displayed with such passion, had at least suppressed her own far less vital worries. She could not claim much importance for her own future, she told herself, at least nothing like as much as this distracted mother claimed for her precious only boy. And then she smiled to herself, for she knew, had never failed to understand, that her own intention, her own motive for this solicitude was, as ever, purely selfish. Totally selfish. In no sense, pure.

Nevertheless she continued to sit with Paula Luccini until the poor woman recovered enough composure to find her ugly little black hat, plant it on her untidy hair, fasten her black coat, spread the knitted top cover over Filippo in his push-chair and get up to go away.

She said goodbye with expressions of gratitude that touched Florence a little, but very lightly. By now she felt more contempt than pity for the woman. Circus folk! Italian – and how! Silly idiot with that big going concern in the family! Why should *she* bellyache about the kid's safety, not yet out of the cradle, not even *sitting up!*

But she shook Signora Luccini's hand warmly and said, 'Shall we meet again? I understand your problem. You may have news. I should like to know what your family decide. I hope so much you will succeed–'

Signora Luccini said, 'You are very kind. If I have good news, perhaps–'

'I will be here again tomorrow.' Florence said firmly. 'I have no friends in Naples, no work, but I love the sea.' She laughed, an artificial sound, but her companion was not disturbed by it. She just repeated her goodbye and hurried away.

Florence wandered into the nearest shopping area, idly interested in what was offered for sale, and how it was presented. She bought a small pre-cooked lunch for herself and passing a stall with foreign as well as local newspapers discovered copies of the continental edition of *The Times*, also a flimsy airmail version of the newspaper of the day before.

She moved back towards the sea front to find a new place where she could rest and enjoy her purchases; the food first, the news later.

This reasonable plan was scattered, destroyed, vanished when she folded the airmail *Times* in half, for as she laid it down beside her to pick up the split roll and salami sausage, she saw a headline that struck her heart and stopped her breath.

'Semi-recluse dies in car crash.'

Below in smaller capitals was another line.

'Wife and child vanish!'

Below that again Florence found the dreadful confirmation of her first shock.

'Mr Percy Bennet, 52, of Garwood House in Dorset was the driver and sole occupant of his Rover car when it smashed into a wall on a narrow lane not far from his home village of Broxbourne. It has not been possible to inform his wife of the accident as she is not at home and her whereabouts, together with that of their only child, a baby boy, are unknown.'

4

Percy dead, instant relief, a thundercloud lifted. But Percy dead, his wife, his heir vanished. His sole heir's death undisclosed, undisclosable.

Florence's first sense of relief changed in a matter of seconds to a mood of despair, for she saw only too clearly how her desertion would be considered. But she continued with her feeble efforts to find work of some sort, keep her professional name for good, live abroad for the rest of her life. Not even able to claim her own belongings, abandoned at Garwood when she fled away in the night, in panic, in grief, in uncontrollable horror at life's essential frailty.

Or could she declare herself now, go to the British Consul with her story and her need? Retrieve her true identity and lay claim to some part of Percy's wealth? God knows he held back her due while he was alive. She could not expect to inherit Garwood House, that would go to the sister he had said he detested. But surely there was a law, wasn't there, about the inheritance of wives?

The word inheritance brought back a clear memory of Percy's rough statement made in their last quarrel. Philip was his sole heir: the property would be in trust for him until he came of age: she would have nothing but what Philip might find in his heart to give her, after he inherited.

Clearly Percy did not expect to live until the boy reached eighteen. But he had died now and the boy was already dead. How could she disclose that, to the Consul, to the lawyers, to the executors? Announce it, and they would want to know why she had not called the doctor at once. Was she mad, or was it true? They would need to see the grave. And the body. Shuddering, she imagined the scene among the bushes in Garwood grounds.

It was impossible. She would rather starve here in Italy, or drown herself in the lazy, dirty blue waters of the bay than confess to the bitter misery of that night.

She began to understand what might have happened had Philip lived. She would have taken him, unhappily but obediently, to the guest house booked for her in Bournemouth. She thought it unlikely that Percy would have paid them a visit there, but he might have telephoned. Perhaps that was what he had done, and finding she had not arrived and that no one knew where she had gone with his son, after leaving home before Gladys came on the morning of her departure, he had dashed off in his own car and crashed it and killed himself in a blind rage.

If Philip had not died she would have gone home with the baby. Or no, she would still have been at Bournemouth, Percy would not have died! It was less than a week since she went away. She was to be at Bournemouth for a fortnight.

Less than a week! No more than five days. Incredible! Percy would not have crashed his car. There would not have been any crisis. Just a repetition of dull unfriendly days, grudging consent to the most reasonable requests.

She shook herself. What was the point of imagining this nonsense. All she had to do to lay a valid claim to money, position, comfort, was to reappear in England with a baby, Philip Bennet. An impossible position? She told herself firmly, *not impossible*. Philip. Filippo. Incredible, but true. Poor distracted Signora Luccini. Paula. Do anything to save her child from being brought up as an acrobat, with all the attendant dangers of that profession. To die, falling from a great height, and all to give enjoyment to a crowd of blood-thirsty, heartless spectators.

That was Paula's fear, her obsession. She, Florence Bennet, needed a baby boy to secure her own future. If she offered the Italian woman a home, education, security, for her threatened child, would she accept it? Could she persuade her to accept?

Florence made up her mind. She had begun the connection without any motive beyond common friendliness. She knew she was going to betray that impulse, use Paula's own false arguments, encourage her mad fears, use them purely to her own use, purpose, her own advantage. A kind of brutal robbery.

But Florence's devious nature allowed her, in self-justification, every possible excuse. In fact she allowed herself to plan the next moves, to follow, if the offer was accepted and the new Philip promised to her. Chief among them, of course, was the money she must pay for her new child.

It did not occur to Florence to feel shame, nor indeed did Paula seem affronted, by this offer to buy little Filippo. She was of peasant origin, used to grinding poverty before she was chosen by her talented husband. In the early days she had been magnificent in jewelled tunic and tights as the stooge handing him the weapons of his act. But the good living that had come to them was still not natural to her, nor the ways, often unkind, of those business Luccinis who had taken such rapid strides in recent years away from circus entertainment. The strange English lady, rich of course and eccentric, as she had been told the English always were, would save this man-child of hers from his fate. Her dreadful fears for him had given her so much pain that she had almost come to hate him. She said as much to Florence when at last she clearly understood what she had been offered.

'He would be safe for always? Even in your cold wet England? Your snow, your fog?'

Florence laughed at her.

'That was a hundred years ago. There is no fog now in the towns. Just white mists sometimes in the country. Where I live is in the south, rolling hills and lovely valleys full of trees and streams and farms with cows and sheep and pigs. Quiet country, with happy farmers and strong children. Filippo will have good friends and go to good schools as he grows up.'

'You can give him all this?'

'I promise you I will do so.'

The battle was nearly won, so far without her needing to produce unconvincing lies, Florence thought. But she was not spared the ultimate question, the final drawing-back.

Staring at her in a culminating agony of indecision Paula said, 'You understand that I love my child. If I give him to you it is for his good only. My husband may kill me for it, unless I leave him. Or set his brothers, the whole tribe of them, on to find him and get him back. They will force me to tell them your name and English address.'

'I will give you neither,' said Florence. 'I

will give you money. Any sum you ask and I suggest you do not try to take advice from anyone or the bargain falls. I should deny this whole conversation ever took place. If you know nothing, they cannot make you tell them anything.'

Signora Luccini was silent for a long time as it seemed to Florence. She was astonished to see, looking at her watch, that it was barely half an hour since they had met. So much the better. She must lose no more time before she reappeared in England in her real name with or without a child, to fight for her inheritance as Percy's widow. It occurred to her, with feelings of dread, that she might easily have several contestants whom he had never even mentioned to her, cousins, possibly bastards. In which case she would have to explain Philip's death. Impossible. Paula must make that impossible.

Florence began to speak again, very slowly and carefully, very very gently.

'I will tell you one more thing, Paula. I understand how you feel about losing Filippo, because I too have lost a child. Oh, I know you are startled. I don't wear a ring. I shall not explain that, nor any more of my own story. But I need the consolation of having a baby again in my arms, to love and care for—'

She went on a bit longer, her recitation lines half remembered from a second-rate,

Victorian play in which she had once acted the part of the fallen woman. Could it have been a dramatic version of the famous *East Lynne?* Quite likely. It always went down famously in the provinces.

When she brought it to an end she saw tears in Paula's eyes and guessed that she had won. Her instinct had not failed her. She had struck the right note.

She covered the necessary pause with her handkerchief pressed to her eyes, only looking up when she felt the Italian woman's hand on hers.

'My poor friend,' she was saying, 'now I do indeed understand. You shall have the boy. He shall be your consolation and I will pray to the Blessed Virgin that he may grow up a credit to us both.'

She seemed to be taking it for granted that the child's future would be known to them both, Florence saw. She swore to her own Protestant God, by habit, not faith, that she and the boy would vanish from Paula's world as completely as if they had never been there.

But she thanked the mother profusely, looked fondly at the baby, but did not touch him for fear a sudden jealousy might reverse the handover conclusion they had just reached and said, 'Paula, this is a great moment, a great decision. You must be quite sure in your mind and heart of what you are doing. I, in my turn, must make my arrangements, buy travel tickets, change travel cheques into cash. I will go first to Rome, where I have friends and where I can get in touch with my home in England. I would like to go by train early tomorrow. So I would like you to bring Filippo, dressed for travel, in this push-chair, which I will buy from you and with the food he is accustomed to have in Italy, to the railway station. When you give him to me I will give you a hundred and fifty pounds of English money, but in lira of course.'

Signora Luccini gasped audibly on hearing this sum spoken, and her peasant's eyes sparkled, showing she was not ignorant of the value of foreign currency. Florence's conscience was still further soothed. After all, she told herself, it was not as if she was cheating the woman. She had every intention of bringing up the child exactly as she promised. She was not really cheating Percy either. She would look after his heir until he came of age, so she would be carrying out the old miser's intention and design of keeping the property out of the hands of the greedy sister and her husband, lying in wait and no doubt at this very moment licking their lips in anticipation of making a kill. A big blow in store for the bloody so-and-sos.

The two mothers, bereaved and about to be so, kissed fondly before parting. Florence watched Paula's short, stocky figure till it turned a corner, then set off herself.

She took some time. The bank was still shut for the midday closing hours and many shops too were in a state of siesta. But she managed to equip herself with a few baby necessities she might be expected to have bought during the last few days, those five days since she left Garwood House in the hour before dawn.

As soon as she could she turned all her travel cheques into cash. After that she found an airline bureau and booked a flight for the next day to Heathrow. This she did, giving her name as Mrs Florence Bennet, with her baby Philip Bennet, also shown on her passport. She had put on her wedding ring for this transaction. The travel office was full of tourists. The girl who served her did not look to see the entry stamp of her arrival in Italy, only showed surprise that she did not have a return air ticket.

'I was in France before,' Florence explained. 'I came to Naples by ship from Marseilles.'

The girl clearly thought this strange behaviour for a woman with a child, but had no time to indulge in idle speculation.

So far, so good. Florence went back to Eleanora's house, with talk of a possible job in Rome. She would be off in the morning. She would go to the station by taxi. She would settle her bill with Eleanora now to save time tomorrow.

The good woman was pleased with the news of her lodger's success. It was unusual, she told Florence, for the whole country was still in a state of turmoil, after the terrible war that had torn it apart. There had been no real recovery. She was both surprised and pleased, she kept repeating.

Florence guessed correctly that the surprise was on account of the money. Perhaps Eleanora had not expected to get it, which spoke well for her good nature and generosity. Perhaps for her gratitude to a country that had taken part in freeing Italy from the enemy and from a failed dictator.

So far, so good, Florence repeated, as she went to her room to re-pack her luggage and prepare for the early start the following day. Before she reached England she must change the baby into a set of Philip's clothes and for this she chose an outfit from the suitcase she had of necessity brought with her, but had not opened since she left Garwood. She put these in the bag she would keep with her in the plane, together with some nappies to replace whatever he would be wearing when she took him. She would have to keep his Italian push-chair until she got to Heathrow. Babies' carry-cots were available on the plane for the flight, she had been told, and had booked

64

one with her ticket.

She was astonished to find herself so calm, so resourceful in her planning, so very determined. She ate, with relish, the favourite meal Eleanora provided, went to bed early and slept without dreaming.

The next morning began well. The taxi arrived punctually; Eleanora hugged and kissed her but did not suggest going to the station to see her off; a move she had half feared for she did not want to hurt the kind woman's feelings.

Arriving in good time at the station for Rome Florence paid her taxi and forced her way into the station concourse, fending off the crowd of boys and men who were attempting to snatch her bags from her. This plethora of porters clung round her until she saw Paula Luccini standing in the appointed spot with the push-chair beside her, staring blankly straight ahead.

The unwanted crowd melted away as the two women greeted one another. The porters were disgusted; the tall, dark foreigner with the strange English, not American, accent, was only a visitor, not a traveller. The more quick-witted turned to run back to the taxi arrival place. Florence and Paula were alone. The Italian lifted an agitated face.

'I *will* look after him,' Florence declared, rising to the moment of drama. 'I will love him with all my heart.'

'Heaven will bless you. May God forgive me.'

There was nothing more to be said. Florence laid a hand gently on the handle of the push-chair. Mrs Luccini took hers from it. The action broke her numbness, but with that her courage. Fear shot up in her eyes as she saw the enormity of what she had done. She turned, but Florence held her.

'This,' she said, pressing the bundle of notes into Paula's shaking hands. The woman stared, then mustering the last of her self-control, pushed the money into her coat pocket and walked quickly away.

Florence waited until she saw Paula pass out of the station. Then she beckoned to one of the fresh group of porters, in a uniform of a sort, who had been watching her short exchange with Paula from a distance.

'I want a taxi to the airport,' she said in her careful Italian. 'You take the bags. I will push the baby. My nurse will join me later.'

She added the last bit to explain the scene she felt sure the man had noticed. He merely grunted and nodded as he picked up the suitcases. There was no trouble in leaving the station.

There was no trouble at the airport. She had planned for and expected a two-hour wait for her flight. She checked in her luggage, including the push-chair and took Philip in her arms now. He was awake, inclined to whimper. She expected no less, but was prepared for it. After all, the good Nurse Barker had shown her, taught her, all she needed to know for when she took charge of this child's predecessor, her own lost Philip.

So she found a Ladies Room, with reasonable provision for the care of young children, and there she managed to take off the rather dirty Italian clothes and put on the clean vest and little warm English outfit she had brought in her carrier bag.

She had silenced the now screaming child with a bottle of his accustomed food and had then found herself a breakfast of coffee and rolls. The plane was ready on time, the flight smooth, easy, and over surprisingly quickly, Florence thought. Mrs Bennet with Baby Philip went through passport control with nothing to declare, no questions asked.

She stood, staring about her, deciding upon her next immediate move. She was on her way, with the heir of Garwood House in her arms, to claim his inheritance.

5

Riding above the clouds that grew ever thicker as her plane drove north across France, Florence decided that her safest plan would be to retrieve her car and drive back to Garwood before revealing herself to anyone. It was going to be difficult. It depended very much how urgently the home need to find her and the child was being pursued.

At Heathrow she was in constant dread of meeting some plain-clothes policeman searching with the help of a photograph. There had not been many on display at Garwood. But there were a few snapshots in the study there.

However, no one accosted her, so she went at once by the airport bus to the Kensington terminal, where she found another meal for herself and was able to give Philip his second feed of the day. Then a taxi took them to Waterloo, where she caught a conveniently quick train to Bournemouth.

All this she managed without asking for help. But now she found her way to the enquiry office, which she knew from past experience was used to dealing with tourists and travellers of all kinds. It was growing dark, though early afternoon, no chance now of getting home that day. But one stage nearer to the car in the garage near Weymouth. She would spend the night in Weymouth.

At Bournemouth there was a train or there was a country bus. She chose the train because with Philip in her arms she would attract attention and be remembered and this journey, the whole journey, must draw no remembered notice.

She had to wait over an hour for the train and it travelled slowly. The daylight had quite gone before she arrived; all the street lights were on. There was no help on the platform; it was not the kind of train that ever needed any. In the rush from the carriage there was no one to help until a middle-aged woman pulled her bags from the rack and humped them out of the train while Florence unfolded Philip's push-chair and fixed him into it. A young man stopped as the woman hurried away; he offered help, so Florence let him take both the suitcases.

'I want a taxi,' she panted, hurrying after him towards the barrier.

'You bloody do,' said the young man, finding the bags heavier than he expected.

Florence was tired, irritated by the grudging discourtesy.

'My car's in dock,' she said coldly.

The young man put the suitcases down at

the barrier and walked away.

Florence handed in her ticket and said as meekly as she could manage, 'Is there a porter anywhere? I can't manage it all by myself.'

The ticket collector laughed.

'Walked out on you, love, did he?'

'He was helping. I didn't know him. I just want a taxi.'

The ticket collector looked surprised, but he called to another uniformed figure, who came nearer.

'Lady wants a taxi, Joe.'

The man picked up the bags and said kindly as they moved away, 'Where to, madam?'

Florence was encouraged to ask his advice. She said she had been touring by car, but it was at a garage and with the baby it was too late to fetch it that day, the works would be shut. Was there a station hotel or some other place suitable for the night? She could afford it, she said, feeling for her wallet.

The porter thought she might be lucky, so did the taxi driver. In the summer she wouldn't have a chance, they said. But this end of the year, not too near Christmas, she ought to be lucky.

She was. She could have a single room with a bathroom in the corridor. She rewarded the porter before she left the station and the taxi driver before he left the hotel.

The receptionist, a white-haired, amiable woman, was sympathetic. Florence signed her name, Maisie Atkins, and put Dorchester as her address.

'I can get the car tomorrow morning,' she explained. 'So I just want bed and breakfast. And a meal tonight. I would like to make up the baby's feed in my room if there's a ring. Or I have a thermos if you could fill it again for me. I've got the food.'

It was apparent that the hotel had very few guests. Several chambermaids came to bring Florence everything she wanted for Philip, in order to see the baby. He was drowsy from travelling, which he seemed to enjoy whenever they were in motion. The chambermaids watched him being changed and washed and fed and offered to look after him while his mother went down to the dining room. Florence accepted their help gratefully. She would be able to ask for it again the next morning when she went to get her car.

She decided not to telephone the garage, though she had kept its name and address. She remembered how and by which road she had come to it on her way to catch the ferry. So she left the hotel with a confident air, leaving her particular chambermaid only too happy to nurse and amuse Philip.

He had cried a good deal in the night and Florence, too exhausted to pay much attention to him, had expected complaints in the morning. But there had been none. Clearly the manageress was too thankful for her custom to put her against the place. Besides, her stay was to be short, provided her car was mended. And her money, perhaps, was short, too, seeing she had not ordered the car to be brought round, but gone after it herself. Not walked out on them, please God, leaving the child.

In less than an hour Florence was back. There had been no trouble retrieving the car. The man in the office said on seeing her, 'Back early, aren't you? Business O.K.?'

'Yes, thank you.'

She had paid for a fortnight in advance and had only had six full days of it. She guessed, and he knew, that there had been no return boat in at Weymouth the night before, but neither referred to it. This time she had remembered to take off her wedding ring before she reached the garage.

'Anything more to pay?' she asked.

'Let's see. Miss Atkins, wasn't it?'

'That's right.'

He made a slow play of opening a ledger and finding the place.

'You paid two weeks' housing and you had a lift in to the ferry with your luggage. Call it evens. Right?'

'Yes. Thank you.'

She ignored the hint about her luggage. She let him bring the car out to the pumps

73

and watched him fill it up with petrol, oil, water for the battery, air for the tyres. She thanked him for his trouble and drove away.

The man went back into his office, puzzled. If this was a smuggling case there was nothing to go on: certainly nothing to report. He was glad he hadn't notified the cops at the start, but she didn't seem right for it. Not like one or two he'd helped the Law with. For a consideration. Well worth it. But no false bottoms or pockets in the car. Nothing unusual but that kid's furniture in the boot. Nothing suspicious about that, either. Strictly her own business. So nothing to report. Good looker, too.

Florence drove the car to the nearest lay-by, unlocked the boot, got out the carry-cot and dusted it off, putting it ready on the back seat. Then she went back to the hotel.

'Proper little angel,' the chambermaid said, disregarding the two tear lines on either side of Philip's little red nose.

She gave the child into Florence's arms and picked up the two bags. Florence carried the baby on one arm and pulled the folded push-chair with the other. In the hall she gave the maid a suitable tip before confirming with the desk that she had settled her bill before fetching her car.

The very young uniformed porter in the hall had watched these proceedings without moving.

'Dick,' the receptionist ordered, but without real compulsion. 'The lady's bags to her car! Now!'

Florence remembered the swarm of competing porters at Naples and nearly laughed. The boy took the suitcases reluctantly, dumped them in the open boot, but without closing it and turned to go.

'Shut that down!' Florence said as she began to settle Philip, now protesting loudly, in his carry-cot. 'And here!'

She held out a shilling, which the boy took awkwardly, muttering thanks.

She wanted to tell him to try a bit harder to please or he wouldn't last for a whole season, but she kept hold of her just annoyance, merely saying 'Shut up!' to Philip, and slamming all the car doors and driving away.

She drove until the child went to sleep again. Then she left the main road for a side one and when she came to a secluded spot on a bend where a wood came down to a small stream, she stopped to get rid of the foreign, and now most unwanted, push-chair. She forced it deep into the undergrowth. Then she drove on.

She had been travelling inland and westward from Weymouth. Reunited with her car and maps she decided to approach Garwood from the west, from Somerset, perhaps. Her story must be quite clear but indefinite. As far as those at the house might expect to be told, she was hurrying back in a state of shock, having spent a few days touring, out of touch with newspapers, until she had found an old one, the day before, with the original announcement of Mr Bennet's accident.

The Garwood staff must be quite new. At least the housekeeper was new. She must ring up and warn the woman of her return.

The housekeeper! She did not know her name! Percy had not given it in his letter. Nor had Mrs Somerton, but perhaps she did not know it either.

Florence stopped the car again in a quiet road, partly to look at the map, but chiefly to discover a village where it would be feasible to ring up Dr Shore.

She chose one with a shop that included the Post Office and had a telephone beside it. The box was intact; even the directories were untorn and in place. It all looked very new. A post-war development, obviously.

She was lucky. Dr Shore was at home and answered in person. It took several minutes to persuade him that she really was Florence Bennet, after which she found it difficult to stop him repeating expressions of sympathy, surprise, pleasure, thankfulness, relief, before he even got as far as asking for Philip.

'Yes, of course he's with me,' Florence protested, half-laughing. 'We're on our way home and we're both fine. Look, I've rung you because I don't know who there is at Garwood. Percy never told me the name of the new housekeeper. I suppose he expected Mrs Somerton to do that. But she walked out on me the day before I left.'

'A Mrs Harper,' Dr Shore answered. 'Threatening to leave every day she gets no news of you. What on earth—'

'I know,' Florence pleaded. 'I'll explain everything. But please, please, be an angel, as you always have been, and ring her up and if you possibly can be at Garwood when I get there, to break the ice with Mrs – Mrs Harper, was it?'

'I've no time for social security ploys,' Dr Shore grumbled. But the short laugh that went with it gave Florence all the assurance she needed.

'Bless you, bless you!' she said softly. 'I'll arrive at three o'clock, unless the car lets me down.'

'It had better not,' Dr Shore told her.

Garwood House, when Florence with Philip, awake but not crying, arrived just after three o'clock that day, was already a scene of great activity. Two men were at work in the garden, figures could be seen at windows on the ground floor and above, polishing the inside of the glass. Dr Shore's car was parked in the drive and the doctor himself stood on the top step by the front door. An active looking woman with neat greying hair stood beside him.

'I told you she'd be on time,' Dr Shore said, raising his hand in welcome but making no attempt to move.

He was an elderly man, turned sixty and looking forward, without regret, to retirement in less than five years' time. He no longer obeyed energetic, physical demands not connected with his profession. So he stayed where he was, though his curiosity and also concern were great. Mrs Bennet had sounded very peculiar on the telephone. Of course the shock of her husband's death must have been great, but her disappearance–? Well, he would soon know.

Mrs Harper, on the other hand, became unusually active. Her face flushed scarlet, she exclaimed, 'Well, I never!' and ran down the steps to the driver's door as the car came to a stop.

'Mrs Bennet?' she panted. 'You *are* Mrs Bennet? The doctor says–'

'Yes,' Florence answered, smiling in relief and pleasure. This was someone she could manage, she realised at once. For the first time since their marriage, Percy had picked exactly the right sort of permanent staff. The first, the only time.

'Yes, Mrs Harper,' she said, switching off the engine, opening the door and leaning back to unlock the rear one. 'Yes, I'm Mrs Bennet and this is Philip.'

She lifted out the carry-cot and put it down on the bottom step. The baby stared up at the two women, his very dark eyes bright in the fading November light.

'Little love,' said Mrs Harper, adding respectfully, 'He has your eyes, madam, hasn't he?'

'Yes,' said Florence.

The elder of the two gardeners came over to help with gathering the luggage out of the boot.

'I shall want both cases and the pram base indoors,' Florence said.

'Put it all in the hall. Lucy will take it up,' Mrs Harper added.

She stooped to pick up the carry-cot. Philip's face crumpled and his mouth opened to scream.

'I'd better,' Florence said. The first thing in the morning, she decided, was to find a nurse for him. If everything was all right. As it was so far.

Everything continued to go smoothly. Though Philip repudiated Mrs Harper, he welcomed the attentions of Lucy, the house-maid, and Dorothy, the cook, who were not related to one another, nor were they local girls, as Gladys had been. They were recently demobilised from the A.T.S. and having served during the war in canteens, had continued to work in what before the war had been called 'service'. 'Do to go on with' was the way they had put it to Mrs Harper when, under Percy's direction, she had engaged them. When he was killed they thought of leaving at once. Only three days on the job and it was in all the papers and Mrs Bennet gone missing, so what was behind it all – best not get mixed up– Well, best wait the week out, Mrs Harper had said and so now she was back, ever so young-looking and the baby and all–

'He'll go to you, Lucy,' Mrs Harper said. 'Mrs Bennet and the doctor will have tea in the study, Dorothy. Yes, now. She looks whacked and no wonder.'

In the study Dr Shore started again with sympathy and worked on towards explanations.

'I've asked Mr Bennet's solicitor to call here at five,' he told Florence. 'He will know exactly how you are placed. I thought I ought to see you first to get a clear account of what you have been doing these last few days. In fact, why you were not at the convalescent home in Bournemouth, had never been there, had, well, disappeared without trace.'

'I suppose I was mad,' Florence said. She had thought out and rehearsed the explanation she meant to give. She must go through it now, making sure she kept it reasonably simple, did not keep adding details that she would not remember later as part of it.

'You know I had – difficulties – with my husband,' she began in a low voice.

He nodded sympathetically.

'I think I ought to tell you,' he said. 'Gladys came to me in a great state the day you walked out on us all, very early in the morning. She said she dared not tell Mr Bennet. Asked me to do it for her. Well, I saw her point. Mrs Somerton had gone, she explained, and you had been alone in the house.'

'And did you get on to Percy?'

'I considered it my duty to do so.'

'Why not the Bournemouth home?'

'I had no idea of its name or address. Percy had arranged it only the day before without telling me. Why should he? I knew of no arrangement or the need for one.'

Florence told him briefly about her quarrel with her husband, about the cause of it, her fears for the child, left to her sole care, his meanness, her exhaustion, need for change, her feeling of repulsion as she considered what the Bournemouth place would be like.

'Old people and mothers like myself at the end of their tethers, ugh!'

'So you decided to go anywhere but Bournemouth,' Dr Shore said, gravely. 'Where did you go?'

This was where the rehearsed script began. Florence bent her head to hide the non-appearance of suitable tears.

'I don't know,' she whispered. 'I think I had a mental breakdown. I drove miles. I stopped at hotels. I hardly spoke to anyone. I just wanted to hide. With Philip. Away from Percy.'

'Your poor husband was frantic,' Dr Shore said. He had been regarding her with disapproval, rather than pity. 'It was–'

He paused, unwilling to spoil her confession by criticism of what he felt was gross misconduct on her part.

'Well,' he went on, more quietly, 'I can't say it led to his car accident, though he did go off in a rage, without Grant to drive him, to Bournemouth when they said from there you hadn't arrived.'

She had lifted her head at the sound of criticism in his voice, but hung it again now.

'It was very wrong of me,' she agreed meekly. 'I shall spend the rest of my life regretting it.'

Dr Shore looked surprised. Florence wished she had left out this very Victorian line. She tried to amend it.

'But I have his son,' she tried. 'I shall do my best to bring him up as Percy would have wished.'

'Indeed I hope you may,' Dr Shore agreed. He still felt perplexed and would have questioned her more closely had not Mrs Harper come into the study to announce the arrival of Mr Bruce McNee.

'Solicitor,' Dr Shore murmured as the lawyer walked in.

Florence had no idea of his existence until that moment. She showed her astonishment and tried to cover it, but both men understood her ignorance, which must explain why her first appeal on her return had been to the doctor.

Mr McNee had arrived with hostile feelings like those of Dr Shore. An unfeeling, unprincipled young woman making unwarranted demands on an ageing husband. Mr McNee was in his early forties and a bachelor. His prejudices were very fixed.

However, he was honest and prepared to support his good client, Bennet's widow, in the management of the estate. He was sole executor of the will, he told a bewildered Florence, but he was able to reassure her about her present position, her future income, the use of the property as Philip's guardian until he came of age.

'Jointly with myself, Mrs Bennet. He is to be brought up here, but you may choose his schools and higher education and choice of profession, if he wishes to follow one.'

Florence was quite willing to leave everything regarding money in his hands, she said. But she must have a nurse for Philip now, a nursery nurse, properly trained.

Mr McNee was surprised to hear she had not got one already. This roused Florence to anger for the first time.

'If Percy had allowed me to keep Nurse Barker I don't think – I don't suppose– He might not– It wasn't *my* fault!–'

She stopped, horrified at her revealing outburst.

The two men exchanged glances, but they said nothing. Very soon they both left. Before going each said she must settle down to make herself a new life with her child: she must apply to them for help whenever she had a problem. She promised to do so.

When they had gone Florence unpacked her bags, throwing all the clothes in the laundry basket. She bathed and fed Philip and then, while Dorothy prepared her dinner and Lucy laid the table and Mrs Harper retired to her own sitting room near the kitchen, Florence unlocked her desk in her own former study and wrote another long cheerful letter to her friend, Amy Tupper. Mainly to counteract the effect of that other letter written less than ten days ago, written from the depth of her misery. It would not do for Miss Tupper to misunderstand her former woe.

Nor, really, her present complacency. But she did not think of that.

PART II

1975, Summer

6

On a summer morning in the year 1975 Miss Amy Tupper turned her car into the drive of Garwood House. Though the visit was in the nature of an emergency call, being in response to a letter she had received only that morning, she felt, as she passed through the ancient arched stone gateway, the familiar warm pleasure at sight of the well-kept lawns and trees that bordered the winding drive to the house.

Twenty-two years, she thought to herself, of peace and quiet, well, nearly always peace and quiet. Nothing like the dreary disappointment of Percy's cheeseparing reign before that. Or the horrors of his maniac search for Maisie and the child, followed by the nightmare of his death. And then the mystery of Maisie's reappearance! Poor Maisie. Poor Florence, rather.

And now what? That letter of today! Just as bad as that old one– Heading for another breakdown?– Surely?–

She had unconsciously accelerated as she drove towards the house, anxious to relieve the anxiety that had been with her from breakfast time; that had stopped her trying to telephone more than once, when she found the number engaged; that had sent her straight out to drive the long miles to Dorset.

'Oh *no!*'

Miss Tupper exclaimed aloud as she drove a good deal too fast round the curve of the drive into the space before the house, causing a young man in the uniform of a police constable to leap out of the way and swing round, scarlet with fright and anger.

'Sorry!' Aunt Amy shouted through the open window of her Mini. 'Didn't expect you!'

Without waiting for his response, she pulled over to where two police cars were lined up: she parked neatly in line with them. Then she got out, forebodings hammering for news.

'What on earth is happening?' she asked the police officer, whose alarm had left him charged with the spirit of revenge.

'You had no business to drive that pace on a private road,' he began. 'I must ask you for your name and business in coming here.'

'Oh, don't be pompous!' Miss Tupper said, tartly. 'I wouldn't have hit you. My brakes are excellent. I didn't expect you, that was all. I've come to see Mrs Bennet. I'm a very old friend of hers. She wrote to ask me over and that it was urgent.'

The constable's face changed.

'You'd better see Inspector Wallace,' he said.

'*But what's happening,* for heaven's sake?' she persisted.

He only said, 'This way, madam,' in a severe, compelling voice and led the way to the front door.

Miss Tupper followed. In the hall she found Mrs Harper, the ever faithful housekeeper, sitting on a chair with a sodden handkerchief pressed to her face. Regardless of her guide, Miss Tupper rushed over to her.

'Oh, Harpie!' she cried, now very frightened. 'What's *happened?* Where's Florence? Is she ill? Why the police?'

Mrs Harper lifted a swollen face and sobbed out, 'I found her – her poor head – the blood – awful!'

'Where is she?'

'I never heard a thing – must have lain there for hours, doctor said– I'll never forgive myself!'

A voice behind them said, kindly, 'My officer tells me you seem to be a friend of the family, madam. May I have a few words with you?'

Aunt Amy straightened herself.

'Indeed you may. You will be Inspector – Wallace, was it he said?'

'Yes. Please come this way.'

Again she was directed, led, moved, into the familiar small room that Florence had used as a kind of office-study; a place where she had by degrees over the years trained herself to manage the affairs of the estate. She had had the help and guidance of Bruce McNee, the family solicitor and the accountant, Cyril Manton, who had advised Percy Bennet between them in preserving the utmost of his fortune from the threatening hand of the tax collector. The estate she held in trust for Philip, until he was eighteen. The two men were in their sixties now, but neither had yet retired.

'This is her office, really,' Miss Tupper said, pointing to the desk. She felt they were trespassing. She swung round and asked again, 'What has happened? You still have told me *nothing!*'

'Please sit down, madam,' Detective Inspector Wallace urged. He had full experience of elderly ladies falling flat out at hearing bad news. But seeing the light of exasperation in this one's eyes he hurried on, 'Mrs Bennet was discovered by the housekeeper at eight o'clock this morning lying on the floor of the lounge near the open french window, with head injuries. She was alive, but unconscious. Mrs Harper telephoned her doctor and us. Mrs Bennet was sent into hospital at once, but they do not hold out much hope for her.'

'She was attacked then, I suppose? Last night?'

'We have no idea of the time. We have not found any weapon here. Dr Armstrong thought four or five hours earlier, perhaps.'

'Before she was found? The early hours, then? The window open, you said. Not forced?'

'No. No damage anywhere. No suggestion of a burglar disturbed at the job. More like a visitor. In fact Mrs Harper says she did have a late visitor last night. Mrs Bennet let him in herself. Told Mrs Harper not to stay up, so of course she went to her own rooms. She has two, a suite as you might say.'

'I know,' Miss Tupper interrupted him. 'I advised her to make a real housekeeper's flat straight off after she got back. That was twenty-two years ago last November,' she added.

'Yes, well. Mrs Harper was naturally curious, because these late-night visits had occurred before at about six-monthly intervals. So she sat by her window till she heard a car in the drive. She is sure Mrs Bennet answered the front door to let in the visitor. It was a man, she thinks. She thinks she heard a man's voice.'

'And he left by the french window?'

'She doesn't know. She sat up for about an hour longer and then went to bed. She sleeps soundly, she says.'

'After a full day's work and she's not as young as she was. I met her first when she'd

91

only been here a few days, in 1953, that was. Youngish then, in her forties, I should think. Brown hair, only a few grey streaks. Florence thinks the world of her.'

'The rest of the staff is local, I gather? Married couple and dailies.'

'Well, the Savins are Polish. They've been here nearly as long as Mrs Harper. They live in the flat over the garage. He drives the car, when she doesn't want to drive herself, otherwise he looks after the garden, with the help of a village boy.'

'Away on holiday,' Detective Inspector Wallace said. 'The two girls are local, I'm told. Change fairly often. The present lot walked in on the crisis this morning and straight out again. I've sent for them, but they've not shown up yet.'

'Typical,' said Miss Tupper. 'Just as the new lot Mrs Harper engaged when Mr Bennet was killed. She got some more from outside, then.'

Wallace nodded, but had no wish to discuss or criticise the bad behaviour of the modern young in employment. He was far too much exposed to their illegal goings-on.

'Now, madam,' he began again. 'We'd better get on with yourself if you don't mind. Old friend of the family?'

'Only of Mrs Bennet,' Miss Tupper answered. 'I knew her over twenty years ago as Maisie Atkins. We were both on the stage and not doing much good there, either of us.'

Wallace let her continue with her memories. She could put him straight on Mrs Bennet's past, stop him trying to find older relatives now all dead, it seemed, and friends, also non-existent apart from local ones.

'I'd left the theatre before her, being older,' Miss Tupper explained. 'But she contacted me when she agreed to marry Mr Bennet, I have the letter she wrote me, asking me to come here to meet him.'

'Which you did?'

'Which I did. Poor Maisie. Stage name, that. Maisie Atkins. Percy, Mr Bennet, made me call her Florence, which was her real name. He was a pain in the neck, that man,' Aunt Amy declared defiantly.

Detective Inspector Wallace smiled, but recalled her to the present.

'You received a call to come here today, I was told. Was that by telephone?'

'No. Letter. I've brought it with me. Also an old one, another sort of S.O.S she wrote twenty-two years ago. On the verge of her breakdown, that was. I thought she might be on the way to another.'

She fished in her handbag and pulled out two envelopes, one yellow with age and bearing the threepenny stamp of that time, the other with the first-class stamp of 1975.

Detective Inspector Wallace took out the

ancient yellow pages from the earlier envelope first. The writing was untidy, but large and reasonably easy to read. After a general description of Percy's meanness over all expenses ever since they were married and an account of their quarrel, only just over, she went on: 'I'm sorry to bother you with all this, but I can't go on and if I don't tell someone about it I feel I might do away with myself, except for little Philip. He depends on me, poor mite, and I'm so hopelessly ignorant about babies and so terrified I may not do the right things. Percy won't let me have a nurse for him any longer. Nurse Barker has been splendid. I felt quite confident while I had her. Now I only have Gladys to help me and she's about as ignorant as I am, except she's got several young brothers and sisters and had helped her mother with bringing them up. Now Percy wants to send me away with Philip to a convalescent home in Bournemouth. All geriatrics, I bet. Perhaps a few squalling infants like poor little Philip. I love him, but when he yells and I don't know the hell why, and I get desperate, I hate him. Wicked of me, I know. What am I to do? What on earth am I to do?'

Detective Inspector Wallace finished the letter and folded it up again.

'What did she do?' he asked.

'I honestly don't know,' Miss Tupper

announced. 'She never went to the Bourne-mouth place. Percy had gone to London before she wrote me that letter, which was the day before she was due to drive herself and the child down. He came back here two days later, rang up Bournemouth to speak to her, found she'd never arrived and blew his top. He found his old housekeeper had left the day before the new one, Mrs Harper, arrived and that Florence had been alone in the house the night before she was due to leave for Bournemouth. Percy was frantic, drove himself all over the place like a madman. Finally crashed his car into a bridge and killed himself. Three days later Florence arrived home with Philip, in her own car, as she had left. With the same luggage. She said she did not know where she had been. That was all she would ever say about the six days she was missing.'

Detective Inspector Wallace drew a deep breath and turned to the recent letter. It was comparatively short. It simply stated that she, Florence, was in great trouble, even danger. It was connected with the time of Percy's death. She ought to have confided the cause to her, Amy, long ago. But for so long there had been nothing to worry about. Now all that was changed. She needed advice, help, urgently. 'Come at once, Amy, if you can. Or it may be too late!'

'Seems like it is too late,' Detective

Inspector Wallace said, handing back both letters.

'The doctor said there was very little hope. What about the hospital?'

'Promised to let us know if there is any change, either way.'

'Then we just have to wait. What about young Philip?'

'Her son? He's on his way. I spoke to him myself when we rang his school.'

'School?' Miss Tupper looked surprised, then smiled. 'Of course. Where he teaches little boys. Prep school. Can't believe sometimes he is that tiny baby and small boy I used to play with when I stayed here quite often to keep Maisie, I mean Florence, company, after she took over this place.'

Detective Inspector Wallace looked at her face some time without speaking. Then he said, 'Up to now we have had no idea at all as to how she got her injuries. Nothing stolen according to Mrs Harper. Nothing damaged. No forced entry. On the contrary Mrs Bennet seems to have had a late-night visitor, according to Mrs Harper and the cigarette ends in the lounge.'

'Not here in the office?'

'You mean the study?'

'Yes, I suppose I do. We called it the office to one another. Only in the drawing room, then? Nothing else? I mean finger-prints?'

One of those, was she, Wallace thought

morosely. Reads crime books and thinks she knows as much about our job as we do ourselves. All the same she was showing herself useful, to say the least.

'It seems to me,' he went on, 'you are the one person who knew Mrs Bennet really well. Of course we are going through all the usual routine. But those letters,' and he pointed to the envelopes still lying in Aunt Amy's lap, 'seem to me to suggest we have to find some incident, some person, connected with her past. Some enemy in fact, looking for revenge, trying to pick a quarrel, losing control–'

Aunt Amy could only nod agreement. This long-winded detective was going to need a lot of prompting if he had any hope of finding poor Maisie's attacker. She wondered if he had ever dealt with this kind of case before.

'I think we have to find what she was up to during those few days she was lost,' she said firmly. 'Can't you discover what happened to her *car* in that time? After all she had it with her. At least she went away in it and she came back in it. And she had the same luggage, didn't she? Suitcases and the baby's pram. It was a carry-cot. Must be here, somewhere; Mrs Harper would know.'

Detective Inspector Wallace was not altogether pleased by this energetic briefing, but it did relieve him of his former feeling of

97

helplessness. He went off to find Mrs Harper, while Miss Tupper, filled now, as often before, by the spirit of the chase, went at once to Florence's desk, to look for its key in the pocket at the back of the top drawer on the right-hand side of the knee-hole.

She found it in the accustomed place and opened the desk. All was in order, as usual. There was no suggestion there that the desk had been used or in any way involved, in that final episode, that tragic ending of a life, full of frustration, anxiety, unhappy failure of promised success. But seeming stability at last. Now, even those twenty-two years of material comfort at least, and surely above all, joy in Philip's progress to manhood, never spectacular, but always steady, were proved to have been no less difficult, no less of a struggle. Why? How?

Miss Tupper locked up the desk again and put the key in her own handbag. She decided to give it to Mr McNee, still Florence's acting solicitor, when he came to the house again that evening.

Mr McNee, now a white-haired, slightly arthritic man, had looked after Florence and Philip with quiet efficiency and kindness ever since her husband's death. It was he who had explained to her the provisions of Percy's will, unamended in spite of the angry man's threats, because he had died too soon. It was Bruce McNee who had looked after the family readjustments when Philip came of age and Garwood became his sole ownership.

Philip was expected to go straight to the hospital on getting the news about his mother, but was not expected to stay if she remained precariously unconscious or more likely had already died. So Mr McNee would meet him at Garwood. Miss Tupper looked forward to seeing him again.

Meanwhile she decided to find Mrs Harper. The poor woman had been too shocked earlier to be asked any questions, and certainly it was not her own business to supplant the detective inspector. But she might be able to give some support, if not comfort, to such a very old friend of the family.

Mrs Harper had made her statement to the Law and had recovered enough to go to the kitchen, where Irina Savin, the Polish cook, subdued but not visibly upset, was sharing her pot of tea with her, while explaining what she proposed to cook for dinner.

'He will be staying here, I suppose, and you will not go away, Miss Tupper, I hope,' she said in her heavily accented English. 'It is a terrible thing,' she added, but the hand pouring another cup for Aunt Amy was perfectly steady.

She had nothing to add to Mrs Harper's

story. The flat above the garage was far enough from the front drive for the sound of cars there to mingle with the traffic on the road several hundred yards away. She and Boris were heavy sleepers. They had heard nothing until Mrs Harper raised the alarm.

Irina Savin was having a calming effect upon the housekeeper Aunt Amy decided, so she talked about herself and recent events in her own life for a few minutes before asking Mrs Harper, as a matter of courtesy, if she might stay the night at Garwood. Philip would like to have her there, whatever the news, she said.

Philip was indeed thankful to find his much-loved Aunt Amy at home when he drove there from the hospital. His mother had died two hours after he got there, without regaining consciousness.

7

Philip Bennet was a strongly built young man, not above medium height, but with the broad shoulders and narrow hips of an athlete. He had very dark, wavy hair and eyes that were black in most lights but sometimes had an amber, even a golden, gleam in them, when he was excited. In the summer he became deeply sunburnt and at all times, though he could be said to get his colouring from his supposed mother, he in no way resembled the father he had been brought up to believe he had lost in his infancy.

Miss Tupper was resting on the drawing room sofa when Philip came in alone, shutting the door noiselessly behind him.

'No, Pip, I'm not asleep. Just resting. It's been a shock for us all. Perhaps the worst for you, my poor boy.'

'I got here as soon as I could. The Head sent me off at once, but driving was slow, holiday traffic pretty thick. We break up in a fortnight.'

'Yes. I know. In any case, she can never have recovered consciousness. Dr Armstrong is sure she didn't come round, try to get help and then relapse.'

'Harpie is still afraid she may have done that.'

'You must talk to Dr Armstrong.'

'I've got to talk to the Law. Detective Superintendent Holmes.'

'I thought it was a Detective Inspector Wallace.'

'Not now she's dead. Now it's murder.'

The dread sound of that word, so familiar in everyday's news, spoken or viewed, silenced them. They stared at one another, Aunt Amy again grey-faced, the young man yellow, his tan faded.

Murder it must be, but why? Who? How was it possible for Florence Bennet, the sad young widow who had devoted herself so wholly to bringing up her only child; for such a secluded, such a locally admired person, to have an enemy evil enough to kill her in her later middle age. It was not only an outrage of an extreme kind, it was difficult to believe it possible. Yet it was true, so it must be explained, the killer found.

Detective Superintendent Holmes, who had joined Detective Inspector Wallace as soon as the news of the death reached the police headquarters, spent the time before Philip's arrival from the hospital in absorbing local colour at Broxbourne village with the Inspector.

Very few facts had so far been gathered.

Mrs Harper's considered account of her discovery, in the official form of a statement, was still highly dramatic, but rather less emotionally rendered. Holmes decided to postpone his interview with Miss Tupper until young Bennet joined her. He thought it might be more productive if he saw the two of them together. Neither had been anywhere near the scene of the crime for several weeks: Wallace had already checked this with the young man's school and with the police, Post Office and local dairy in Miss Tupper's home village in Kent.

So, with a regrettably empty mind and looking for maximum assistance, he asked Philip and his Aunt Amy to join him in the study.

'Complimentary aunt, no real relation,' Miss Tupper explained and gave a brief account of her long friendship with the boy's mother.

'You speak of two so-called crimes,' Holmes said. 'This trouble with her husband–?' He stopped, glancing at Philip.

'All about money,' the young man said. 'I was told about it when I came of age. By mother first, and then by our solicitor.'

'That would be Mr Bruce McNee?'

'Correct. He's quite an old boy now, but as spry as ever. He drew up the original will.'

Aunt Amy intervened.

'Mrs Bennet was kept in ignorance of the terms of that will when it was made. She heard them from her husband the night they quarrelled and she decided to leave him, with Philip. Then when she read of Percy's death in an accident and came back, she got in touch with her doctor at that time.'

'Old Shore?' Philip interrupted. 'I remember him when I cut my leg on the glass at the top of the church wall.'

'You were ten at the time,' Aunt Amy confirmed. 'You had a tetanus injection.'

'Mrs Bennet got on to her doctor, name of Shore?'

'Dead now. It's Armstrong, but he'd have the old notes of the firm, wouldn't he?'

'Certain to.' Detective Superintendent Holmes began to regret joining Aunt Amy to their interview. 'But I want to know about the solicitor, Mr McNee, at the time of your father's death, I think you said, Mr Bennet?'

'That's right. But mum had told me the place was mine from the start. In trust with the solicitors; all that jargon. Not important. I'd never let her down. I was very fond of her.' His voice broke a little as he said this, but his face hardened. He was not going to break down before a cop.

'It may be jargon,' said Holmes, gently. 'But it might be the cause of envy, jealousy and malice. Were there no contestants of the will?'

'I was a few months old. I wouldn't know.'

Again Aunt Amy came up with intelligent information.

'Neither Florence nor Percy had many surviving relations,' she said. 'Florence's parents were dead: I don't know how or by whom she was brought up. I never heard of any relations or friends either, except fellow actors and stage people. But Percy did have a married sister in Canada. A business man, I think. One son, but not a Bennet.'

'Thorntons,' Philip said, recovering the initiative. 'They came here one summer holidays, when I was at prep school. Father, mother, my aunt, girl about my age, bossy little bitch, boy younger, drank too much cider at lunch and was sick in the kitchen garden later.'

'Poor child,' said Aunt Amy. 'You were bullying him, I suppose.'

'I wasn't. I was up my tree, getting away from them.'

Detective Superintendent Holmes intervened.

'Was this the Thorntons' only visit?'

'No. They're supposed to be coming over here again, this year. May be in the country by now. Before this they came scuttling over for my birthday when I came of age, to see what I meant to do with this place now it belonged to me outright.'

'When was that?'

'Four years ago. Legally – we had a real do when I was twenty-one last year.'

Holmes continued with a painstaking string of questions relating to Philip's schooling, his three years at a redbrick university, his modest degree, his present position as a junior assistant master at his old prep school in Hampshire.

A very ordinary middle-class education, the detective considered, followed by a surprisingly tame occupation for one whose only talent appeared to be for games and athletics. And of these jumping and indoor gym on apparatus seemed to be the high spots. In this field he had won prizes at school and college.

'So you teach little boys to "flop" their own heights?' Holmes asked, smiling.

Philip coloured, his dark eyes sparkling.

'Some of them are really good. At their age, the under-thirteens, they are never frightened. They don't argue. They want to get it right. Not only to show off.'

Miss Tupper was surprised by that instant flash of anger. He was obstinate, she knew, but in a quiet way, like Florence, who seemed always to be meek and nervous, but was really one of the most determined women she had ever known. But never like this; quick anger, instant defence.

Detective Superintendent Holmes changed the subject, returning to the question of the

Thorntons from Canada.

'These relations of yours. You say you think they may be in England now. Did your mother tell you this or did they get in touch with you to arrange a visit?'

'They wrote to my mother. She mentioned it in her last letter. Something about the feud being over, or she hoped it was over. She didn't seem to be upset by the idea, or worried at all.'

'But she wrote of a feud. Does that mean a continuing family quarrel?'

'Not an open one. She always thought they might be a danger to *me.*'

'*Danger?* How?'

'Well, father married very late, didn't he?'

'Fifty,' Aunt Amy said. 'So Philip's arrival did upset their very long cherished expectations.'

'Thank you,' Holmes told her, with anything but a grateful look, while Philip stared at the floor, wishing she would go away. Much as he loved her, as a generous presence all his childhood, he wished he could be, and be seen to be, the sole guardian of the family affairs and possessions: the sole voice in the conduct of Garwood's future.

'Your mother may have been afraid your father had left the Thorntons completely out of his will?' Holmes asked, looking directly at Philip.

'Indeed she was, and told me so when they

came to my eighteenth birthday party. You see, they had relied on the only will they knew of, which gave them everything. My father did let them know he had married and that I had been born the next year, but he did not tell them of the new will. They must have guessed there was one, but as he had not mentioned it to them, they were not going to put the idea in his head for him.'

'People are often careless about that sort of thing. You'd hardly believe how careless they are,' Holmes told him.

'I suppose so. Anyway, they were pretty furious when they knew, after my father's death, that they were not even mentioned in the new valid will, made after his marriage. The visit twelve years later was the first move they made. More to see if Garwood was being kept up properly and me too, I suppose. They were still next heirs weren't they? Even if not mentioned in the will?'

'I expect so.'

'And they came four years ago for the same reason, I think. To inspect the property and see what I looked like "of age". They themselves looked quite old to me. Neither of the brats came. Not interested. They wrote to my mother about the present visit, not to me. Ought to have done really. I don't know why not. Nor why mother gave me no date or where they would be staying. Just that they were coming over and it worried her.'

Detective Superintendent Holmes turned to Miss Tupper.

'That letter Mrs Bennet wrote to you. Nothing about the Thorntons in that, was there?'

'*Letter!*' Philip shot an infuriated glance at Aunt Amy. She opened her bag and handed, almost threw, the summoning letter to him.

'Keep it,' she said. 'Unless Mr Holmes wants it.'

The officer shook his head.

'No, Mr Bennet here had better have it,' he said. 'You had better both know that a Mr Thornton and his son have taken rooms in Dorchester and have already made an appointment to see your Mr McNee, who informed me of this an hour ago. He, Mr McNee, will be in touch with you shortly.'

'*Now!*' said Philip violently, springing to his feet.

'Just a minute first, sir,' Holmes said, with such compellingly polite firmness that Philip sat down again. 'According to Mr McNee the Thorntons have come over to discuss the whole question of the inheritance again. They have been in Broxbourne recently, putting up at the Puddle Arms, I think the pub is called.'

'Piddle,' Philip said, hoping to confuse the police officer. Failing in this he explained. 'The other river. Piddle. Puddle belongs to the martyrs.'

'So I have always understood,' Holmes told him politely. 'In any case their object in visiting the village seems to be in order to investigate certain vague rumours that have come to them regarding the Percy Bennet family.'

'Such as?' Philip, not at all modified by his failure over the rivers, still spoke and stared angrily.

Detective Superintendent Holmes got up to go. He fully understood the young man's indignation over the Thorntons, father and son. Their persistence, their interference, especially now, in circumstances they could not have foreseen when they planned this latest visit, must add to young Bennet's anger and grief. And also to the very demanding police search for a murderer.

'I would rather leave the Thornton angle to Mr McNee, sir,' he said. 'You have been into it before with him, I understand, so it will be for him to fill you in on this latest move.'

'You don't think one of them was the late-night visitor to my mother and lost his temper?'

'I have no opinion at all on those lines,' Holmes insisted. 'But of course we are continuing to look for that visitor and discover his identity.'

'Pompous ass!' Philip exploded, while the detective was still at the now open door.

He was still there because Mr McNee was just coming in. So it was he who received the full vehemence of Philip's criticism.

'Meaning me?' he asked cheerfully, coming into the room.

'Of course not, you old ass!' Philip said, grinning at him with affection. Then, seeing the look of horror on Aunt Amy's face before such flippant rudeness, he muttered, 'The Law. Mean well, but these up-stage coppers. Throw the book at you. Pass the buck. No action–'

'Nonsense!' Mr McNee was indulgent, but firm. 'They do marvels with modern electronics in the way of organising arrests, following suspects and communicating with each other. Real-life ploys, streets ahead of most of the thriller writers.'

'But you are to tell us about the goings-on of the Thorntons, so Mr Holmes said,' Miss Tupper broke in. 'Florence thought all that nonsense had faded when Pip took over the management of the estate four years ago. Why are they here now and what do they want this time?'

The solicitor said, without hesitation, 'They were encouraged to come by a letter suggesting Philip here is not the true heir, because he is not the eldest of Mr Percy's sons.'

'Then who the hell *is* the eldest?' Philip burst out violently.

'I know that,' was Aunt Amy's instant response. 'The old housekeeper, Somerton, had a bastard boy she always said, quite openly, was Percy's. She also said, and tried to maintain at the time of Percy's marriage to Florence, that she had been legally married to him. But she never tried to take it to court and he always denied the whole claim. The marriage to Florence was certified as true and so was Philip certified as Percy's only legal son and inheritor of the whole estate.'

Philip listened to all this with a stony face and only said quietly to the solicitor at the end of it, 'Is that old woman, what's her name, Somerton, still alive?'

'I believe so,' Mr McNee told them. 'The bastard son is a bad doer. Juvenile Courts. Borstal. Must have been at one of the old approved schools when you were born, Philip. Mrs Somerton kept her so-called wrongs to herself then. I'm sure Mrs Bennet knew nothing of it. There's nothing to show whether she did or not in the records. Either at the time of the marriage or at Philip's birth and the signing of the new will. Much later on Mrs Somerton came to me with her story and I silenced her. Told her it simply would not wash and she hadn't a case. Young Reg was in prison at the time.'

'So this story got to the Thorntons in spite of you and they are trying to make it stick, are they?' Philip said.

'The Thorntons have been to see me,' Mr McNee agreed. 'They consider my firm kept the whole affair too hidden by half. It seems they have been snooping round Broxbourne, talking to all and sundry at the Piddle Arms there. With this dreadful attack on Mrs Bennet—'

Philip said, 'If they came to argue with my mother and the young one, I never knew his name, they called him "Tig" or some such shit, hit out at her— Sorry, Aunt Amy.'

'Very unlikely,' she said smartly, ignoring the language and the apology for it. '*Not* the way to get hold of the property. What they are looking for is a previous marriage. Isn't that it, Mr McNee?'

'It could be and as far as the Somerton family is concerned there is nothing doing whatever.'

'So let us hope they'll take themselves back to Canada pronto,' said Philip. 'I don't want them here at any price.'

Which put a thought in Aunt Amy's head.

'What about me?' she asked. 'Can I be any use now or shall I go home?'

'Stay,' said Philip. 'I need you more than ever I did when you wheedled mum into letting me have my own way. Poor old mum.'

His voice broke again and he fished for his handkerchief.

Mr McNee put together the papers he had

taken from his briefcase.

'The postmortem will be done this evening,' he said. 'And the inquest fixed as soon as possible. Come down to my office in the morning, Philip. I may have more to tell you. The police are on the track of this late-night visitor. Bert Elbury at the pub may be able to help them there. I gather there have been other strangers in Broxbourne recently besides the Thorntons.'

'I'll stay as long as you need me, Pip dear,' said Aunt Amy. 'I'll go to Harpie now and see if she's fit to talk yet. Irina is quite calm and making dinner for us. You'll want to ring your school, I expect.'

She left the two men together. McNee was glad she had done so. He had advice to give his young client and various things to tell Philip that were not at all Miss Tupper's business.

He was over forty years older than the young man, who knew very little as yet of the ordinary dreary ways of life in this over-crowded, modern, so-called civilised state. Facts about the conduct and formalities associated with death and burial. Facts about responsibility in sudden death, above all, about crime. There had been matters concerning Garwood and its owners that had come the way of McNee's firm. He had known this boy from the time of his birth. He had known Percy Bennet as a young man. Not a nice young man, but one given to unpleasant scrapes from which he had to be rescued by means of bribes. Percy had been open to blackmail far too often, though nothing serious had emerged since his death to assault his young widow. Nothing that is, to date. But there was always the possibility that something of the sort was rearing its ancient wicked head now and having failed had struck fatally and might strike again.

These facts and surmises and warnings were for young Philip Bennet's ears alone.

8

With his mind on Mrs Bennet's past as the only possible clue to her killing, other than the inevitable 'strange' robber, Detective Superintendent Holmes suspended further work at Garwood and set out to find and interview old Mrs Somerton. He chose her just because she was now so old and he was afraid this fresh calamity in the Bennet family might carry her off. But also because she had known Percy Bennet far longer than anyone else in Broxbourne.

He found her living in a semi-detached villa, neighbour to her youngest niece, who had a husband and two children. She looked well, robust, stout, not very active, but she gave the impression that she looked after this family rather more effectively than they looked after her. She was perfectly willing to talk about the Garwood people as she called them.

'Mr Percy's grandfather it was made the family fortune,' she explained. 'Which his son, Mr Percy's father, took a delight in throwing the best part of it away. There was but the one son, Mr Percy, and one daughter, who married into a Canadian family, name of Thornton.'

Her small eyes watched Holmes carefully as she spoke. Did he know this sister's people were over just now? Just before this terrible deed, this just retribution, this defeat of her twenty-four-year-old enemy? She saw that he did and that he was going to question her knowledge.

'I understand,' Detective Superintendent Holmes said, 'that you were Mr Bennet's housekeeper for a number of years. In fact from the time of his father's death to that of – well, a few days before Mr Percy himself. Will you give me your version of that misunderstanding or series of misunderstandings between members of the household.'

As Mrs Somerton continued to stare, without speaking, Holmes went on cautiously, 'Mrs Somerton, I don't for a moment wish to pry into your private affairs, which can have only an indirect bearing on what happened last night or early–'

'Indirect bearing my aunt fanny!' exclaimed Mrs Somerton, fiercely. 'When my only son, that wicked man's eldest, went unsupported and uncared for, ten years or more. To the eternal detriment of his upbringing, and me still slaving for him, the boy's father, more fool me! Putting up with the trouble and shame of his wildness and his bad ways–!'

'You need not distress yourself over Reg's

conduct to me, Mrs Somerton,' Holmes told her. 'We do know his unfortunate history, but he seems to be settling down at last, doesn't he?'

'No credit to his father for that. Nor to her, neither. Running off, the Lord knows where, and lost best part of a week. It's my belief if Mr Percy had not died she never would have come back. There's plenty of others in Broxbourne think the same.'

This was the rumour the detective super-intendent had already met with in several guarded versions. He wanted to get the details more clearly but he had already decided that Mrs Somerton was so riddled with hatred of Mrs Bennet, jealousy of her position as legal widow of the man she had grown to consider her husband, that he hesitated to ask any more direct questions.

Mrs Somerton, however, was well and truly started upon the full treatment of her case. She was not ready to let it drop just yet. Lawyers had been putting her off for years, not wanting to know the full injustice of her sad story. Yet here and now this high-ranking copper was only too anxious to know all she could tell him. Percy and his young, so-called wife were now both dead, but *she* wasn't. Nor was Reg. If she could black that stupid, soft-spoken, obstinate supplanter, she would do so and enjoy the doing of it.

'It's my belief,' she said, leaning towards Holmes and speaking in a low, urgent voice, 'that she left Garwood with that child of hers, meaning never to come back, perhaps to get it adopted. She'd been making scenes ever since the monthly nurse left, because she didn't want the care of the child and he expected her to look after it. She has never said where she went those six days. It's my belief we never would have seen her again, nor the child either, only Mr Percy killed himself in one of his rages. Then back she comes, with the baby, *if it was the same one.*'

Detective Superintendent Holmes was astonished.

'Why not the same one? What an extraordinary idea! Don't you think that's a very peculiar suggestion, Mrs Somerton? Well, rather an unbalanced one?'

Mrs Somerton was bitterly disappointed. The drama she had invented and then nourished and developed over the years, chiefly to support her fantasy regarding Reg, had grown both hard and fixed. She had come to believe it highly possible and probably true. Her neighbours in the village, without actually believing in it, were aware of it as a dark, though still small shadow over Garwood House. But when Philip came of age they were very willing to accept him, rumour or no rumour.

Now, with a new kind of dark shadow,

more sinister than the disposal of a baby boy, perhaps his adoption and then his recovery, or if not the same child, another in his stead, the whole story seemed to be splitting apart, the true and the false equally astonishing, equally reprehensible. Above all, somehow shameful, sordid, unworthy.

How had such a tale been invented, Holmes wondered, as he drove away from Mrs Somerton's ugly little villa. Jealousy, spite, disappointment over the young tearaway, Reg? Old age confirming a memory? More than usual housekeeping abilities, or Percy Bennet would never have kept on his mistress after she had produced the evidence of their relationship.

No. He had wanted an heir. It would be like him to wait until the unwanted child showed he had the right qualities for the post. If Reg had turned out well, Percy would have married the Somerton young woman, in spite of her age, for she was several years older than he was. The title and surname were traditional to the office of housekeeper. There had never been a Mr Somerton.

When Reg proved a hopeless failure, Percy had looked for a wife and found a girl who could fill the bill. And said so. But he knew next to nothing about her. He dismissed Somerton, who was on the point of walking out on him anyway. He lost his heir's mother, because he had never thought of her as anything but a child-producing machine. No wonder the whole business was sordid, shameful.

But the answer to Mrs Bennet's murder must still lie in her past, Holmes concluded, not in village gossip promoted by a half-crazy old woman. Perhaps in the distant past. And to reach that he must unravel the mystery of that lost week. Mrs Bennet, being dead, could not help him. Philip, four months old at the time, could not help either. But the car, that little old second-hand Austin, had it no signs on its return, to suggest where it had been or what it had been doing? Boris Savin, the chauffeur gardener, had given him the address of Mr Grant, the man he had succeeded. Grant had been chauffeur to Mr Bennet for some twenty years, retiring at the early age of fifty-four, a couple of years after his master's death. If anyone in the district could help over the car, Grant would be the man.

Detective Superintendent Holmes drew up outside the Grants' filling station on the Bere Abbas road out of Broxboutrne. It was a self-service station, with an efficient girl in the office and a round-shouldered, long-haired boy hovering near the pumps, able, but less than willing, to help those who could not manage to help themselves. Holmes knew that Grant was now in his seventies and did not expect to find him at work. He did not have any trouble in reaching him, however. The girl was a granddaughter, who jumped up at once when the detective explained who he was.

'You can see granddad here now, if you like,' she said. 'He comes down twice a week to look at the books and see we're not putting away a fortune on the side.'

'Present prices being what they are,' said Holmes, smiling.

Old Mr Grant did not leave his chair when the detective superintendent appeared in the small neat room behind the office-showroom. But he waved a hand towards a thermos flask and a group of mugs on the table beside him.

'Help yourself, officer. You'll be wanting to ask me about poor Mrs Bennet, I reckon. Never had much luck that one, did she?'

'I wouldn't know,' Holmes said. 'Thank you, no,' he added, as Grant waved his hand again to the thermos flask. He went on, 'My enquiries are bogged down over that six days she was missing, around the time of Mr Bennet's fatal car crash. She was in her own car, I believe. Can you vouch for that?'

'Seeing I was with the Daimler in London with the master I only know for certain her Austin was in good running order when we left Garwood and she came back in it three days after Mr Bennet's smash. With the little master, of course, and his gear.'

'The Daimler was a write-off?'

'Oh yes. Mrs Bennet got the insurance money, but she didn't want to see the poor old wreck. Kept his cars till I refused to drive them. Mean in everything, that one.'

'Nothing wrong with the Austin?'

'Oh no. But then there can't have been much chance of that.'

'What do you mean?'

'Well, I'd give it a dust over a couple of days before I left with the Daimler and she was due to drive to Bournemouth. I always checked the oil and water and tyres and had a look at the mileage, to know when an oil and grease was needed.'

'Full maintenance, in fact. You serviced both cars, I suppose?'

'That's right. Well, as I was saying, I'd made a mental note of the mileage the last time. She hadn't been using it much the last few months on account of having the baby, you understand. So when she came back I checked it all over again and she'd not gone above a hundred or so all told.'

This was valuable news indeed. Those six days touring looked more like a single visit and that to somewhere not above fifty miles from Broxbourne and back. No continuous travel, no touring. She had lied to Miss Tupper, evidently. And yet Miss Tupper was her oldest and most intimate friend. *Where had she been?* Where had the Austin stood unused? If quite near home why had no one seen it about on short trips here and there? For no one had come forward to report this. Perhaps it was too soon to expect Wallace to have any news in this respect.

'Just one more question, Mr Grant. Or rather, two. Can you remember the registration number of the Austin? And did you ever see its log book?'

The old man gave a short laugh.

'Number, yes, indeed. Never forget numbers of cars. Only the names of their owners.'

He gave the Austin's registration without any hesitation, pointing out that Mrs Bennet must have bought it second-hand before she married Mr Bennet, for she came with it and used it afterwards, but only for shopping and visiting her friends. He had never seen the log book.

'Did she keep it on after she came back to Garwood?'

'Only a month or two.' Mr Grant leaned forward to speak in a lower tone. 'And that was a queer caper, if you ask me, officer. She comes to me one morning and says, "Grant, I want you to get me a new car. I want a good one, but not too big. One I can drive myself and take Nanny and the baby about as he gets older. Not very expensive, not a Rolls or a Daimler, but a good reliable make. British, not American."'

'What did you get her?'

'A Vauxhall. That was back in '53. I left the job not long after. But she's had a good many car changes since, of course. Rover mostly. Good, careful driver for a lady. Never messed them up. Not above a turn of speed. Cool head in a crisis, that one.'

Mr Grant was tiring; his voice was getting hoarse and his attention was flagging. Detective Superintendent Holmes knew he must bring the interview to a close.

'Well, thank you very much indeed, sir, for a most useful piece of evidence,' he said, getting up to go. 'Oh, just one more thing. What happened to the Austin? Did you get rid of that for her? Who to? Where?'

'Blest if I know! I had nothing to do with that. May have give it away, for all I know. I did wonder a bit at the time. She went off in it one day and came back in a taxi. When I asked her if she'd been in any trouble in it she just laughed and said no, she'd sold it, no point in having two cars for one person. It was that, more than anything else, gave me the hint my time was up or nearly so. I'd had my eye on this place, very good position it is for Broxbourne folk, so I give in my notice before she put her mind to speaking herself.'

'Good for you, Mr Grant,' Holmes told him gravely.

There was plenty for the detective

superintendent to consider as he drove to his temporary office in Broxbourne, now called the Incident Centre by the press.

According to the old chauffeur Mrs Bennet had lied when she spoke of touring for six days. Her car had not travelled more than one hundred miles all told. Down to the coast, the Dorset coast, and back? To a resort? Lyme? Weymouth? *Weymouth!* Abroad? With a four-month-old infant? Unlikely. But well worth a few enquiries. Better put this problem to Miss Tupper. Hers was the only memory that operated over the whole period and before 1953 into the bargain.

Miss Tupper began by doubting the accuracy of Grant's statement, especially about the figures on the mileage gauge. About the car number he was probably right, she said, when Holmes read it out to her.

'It does sound familiar, though I wouldn't swear to it. But she had the car already; before her marriage, second-hand, cheap, I mean. Difficult to get anything new, even in 1953. This was quite old. Got it from a friend who couldn't afford to keep it. Nor could Florence, really, but she was engaged to marry Percy. Blackmailed him into coughing up the wherewithal, I expect.' Miss Tupper chuckled gently, then added, 'So it would have been registered in her maiden name, or more likely still in her stage name,

Maisie Atkins.'

Holmes remembered that Grant had never seen the Austin's log book. Now Miss Tupper was suggesting a still wider search relating to that missing week in the life of the murdered woman. Mrs Bennet and her infant son, lodging perhaps on the Dorset coast, or that of Normandy, Brittany, or the Channel Islands and an ageing, little, late 'thirties Austin registered in the name of Maisie Atkins, spinster, or perhaps, less likely, Florence Bennet. In either case the address ought to be Garwood House, Broxbourne. Though why she had not altered the name was a mystery.

'Why more likely, Miss Tupper? Wouldn't it be natural to renew the licence in her married name when she altered the address? Do you happen to remember what address she would use when she acquired the car in the first place?'

'Afraid not,' Miss Tupper answered. 'But quite like her. Rather lazy, really. All right in a crisis, kept her head. But she'd go to any length to avoid trouble for herself.'

'Mr Grant said much the same about her driving,' Holmes told her.

She laughed.

'Grant! Splendid person. Only member of Percy's staff he couldn't impose on, either by his meanness or his cruel tongue or his shocking temper if roused.'

Detective Superintendent Holmes called in at the Piddle Arms before he left Broxbourne that evening. Detective Inspector Wallace had been recalled to take over another case, leaving a detective sergeant, Tom Miles, as assistant to Holmes. Miles stayed at the Incident Centre to take messages of any kind and relay them as needed.

Holmes had intended to have a quick beer only, while making himself known to the landlord, Bert Elbury, and any other regulars who happened to call in the first hour after opening.

Rather to his surprise the bar was empty except for Elbury himself, who put down the glass he was polishing and leaned forward to say in an interested voice, 'You don't remember me, do you, Mr Holmes?'

'Should I?' The detective put on his regulation genial smile while searching his memory without success.

'Case of arson at the village school, all of ten years back. You were Sergeant Holmes then, I seem to recollect.'

'Quite right. And you weren't landlord of the Piddle Arms, either. Uniform. Army. Home on leave. Right?'

'Right. Had a lift to the corner on the main road and was walking down when the blaze went up and that young lout ran straight into my arms, looking back at what

129

he'd started. Just after midnight it was.'

'Of course, the neighbours got it under control before the fire brigade arrived. You were hanging on to a very scared young villain and there was a hell of a lot of water but no fire. *And* the lad was Reg Somerton. Caught red-handed, his first offence if my memory serves.'

'First convicted offence,' Elbury corrected. 'Well known already in Broxbourne for vandalism and nicking things like bicycle pumps and lamps, letting down motor bike tyres, throwing stones through windows. Spoilt from birth. No father, you see. Least-ways– What'll it be, sir?'

Holmes ordered his beer and offered one to this long unmet acquaintance. He led the conversation to other strangers who had visited the village recently. Elbury did not want to go on discussing the petty criminal, Reg Somerton. Besides, he seemed unlikely to share his mother's feelings over the Garwood inheritance. Too low an intelligence, too intermittent a member of Broxbourne village, to keep up with its history or its development. Too low altogether to attempt blackmail.

'There was those Thorntons from Canada,' Elbury said thoughtfully. 'I take it you're looking for someone with a grudge against Mrs Bennet. I reckon the young one they call Tig might lose his temper with the

130

lady. She was getting well into middle-age and a bit short-tempered. But Mrs Harper thinks it was some gentleman visitor that'd been before, lateish.'

'Yes? This is common knowledge or perhaps speculation, hereabouts, isn't it?'

'Ideas get about in a crisis. There has been a stranger, comes in for a bite and a whisky now and then, just before closing time. Very cagey. Never says where he's from, or where to. About every six months this last year or two. He was in night before last, I recollect.'

Detective Superintendent Holmes looked at the landlord steadily for a few seconds. Then he said, 'You wouldn't have noticed the number of his car, would you, seeing him off *after* closing time?'

'No head for figures, Super,' Bert Elbury said, shaking his head. 'But the letters was local. Ford, Volvo, oldish style, light grey or beige. I disremember which.'

There could be a connection, Holmes decided. A stranger with a local registration.

So much for the visitor. And his car. Could be traced, perhaps. But that other car? Better not even mention it to Elbury. What could he be expected to know, or to remember an Austin of twenty years ago. What a hope! Must be sunk without trace!

9

The inquest on Mrs Bennet was opened two days later, at which the cause of death was accepted as fracture of the skull with consequent brain damage, resulting from a blow with a blunt instrument given by a person or persons unknown. Police evidence was wholly negative. No weapon had been found: there were no suspects under investigation. The inquest was adjourned with permission for burial.

The funeral was arranged for the following Friday at Broxbourne church, where the latest Bennet to die shared a plot with her forebears. Percy's grave was open to admit his wife, whose tragic, violent death was genuinely regretted by the villagers. She had been consistently kind and considerate to a long succession of village girls who had submitted, with varying success and achievement, to Mrs Harper's excellent training. Most of them had not stayed above a year and had moved on to a great variety of jobs they favoured. But they had learned, those who stuck it out, to gain some regularity of living, healthy meals, not all snatched out of the freezer, but collected from the kitchen garden and the hen-run and the butcher's shop. Girls who had worked at Garwood surprised the Broxbourne men whom some of them married, by their cooking and other household skills. So it was not surprising that the little church was filled to over-flowing for the funeral. Unfavourable rumours were set aside. Young Mr Bennet had been brought up very well: he was a credit to all who had had a hand in it. He didn't take after old Mr Bennet in looks or build, far from it, but he had his mother's colouring and a handsome face.

Garwood, being nearly two miles from Broxbourne and still more or less dis-organised, with the police making tests and searchings, the village hall was used for tea and refreshments after the burial. The Canadian family had been in touch with Philip before the inquest, which they did not attend. But he had invited them to the service and they came, shook hands at the graveside, but left immediately after that.

No other Bennet connections appeared or had made themselves known. Florence had none to represent her side of the family. Only Aunt Amy was there to act as hostess at the modest funeral feast. It was in most minds that young Philip (only the oldest inhabitants thought of him and called him 'the young master') would be marrying before long and come home to run the place, give up his teaching, no doubt. Some people had all the luck. Well, perhaps it wasn't very lucky to have your mother bashed on the head and killed; and he already had the place, of course.

Mrs Somerton did not attend the funeral. Reg was not at home, nor on strike this time, as he often was. His mother could not say what he was up to. He had not let her know. The village had not seen him recently.

It was nearly two years since Reg Somerton was last inside, Detective Superintendent Holmes reflected, on his way to the Incident Centre later that afternoon. In any case, cold-blooded, deliberate murder of an ageing woman, seemingly unconnected with robbery, was outside Reg's very limited former range of misdoing. Besides, the Weymouth force had come up with a character who had been one of their informers on smuggling crimes for years. Retired now, but very active twenty years ago or more. Knew that field like nobody's business and always kept an eye and an ear open at that holiday resort and small port for Channel crossings. Holmes had taken the name and address, which was that of a garage the man owned and still ran, just outside the town. Without much hope, the detective decided to look him up. About the Austin to start with. Later perhaps about his possible visits to the Piddle Arms. In the man's own car, an old make of Ford, perhaps, grey or fawn, with a local registration number too

On the day after the funeral Philip went back to his school and Miss Tupper to her cottage in Kent. Mrs Harper agreed to stay as housekeeper and the Savins, who saw no possibility of finding any other home or work in England and were profoundly shocked at the mere suggestion that they would like to leave, promised to look after the garden and the Rover until Mr Philip made up his mind about his future.

He was only twenty-two, but he was a very rich young man. Mr McNee went back to Garwood after the funeral guests had all gone home and the tea helpers, Garwood staff and Broxbourne villagers had cleared everything away and been generously rewarded.

At Garwood Mr McNee suggested a private interview with Philip, but the latter insisted that Miss Tupper be present.

'Well, yes,' Mr McNee agreed. 'Perhaps Miss Tupper was in Mrs Bennet's confidence on money matters all along.'

'Not a bit of it,' Aunt Amy protested. 'Not a word from first to last.'

'Then you won't know that over the years, from very careful handling of the care and upkeep of the property and most sober, but not abstemious, living on her own part, though she spared nothing on your education, Philip, she managed to save a personal fortune of no mean order.'

'Did she indeed!' Aunt Amy said, quite amazed by this unexpected disclosure. 'Now why did she do that?'

'How splendid of her!' her son exclaimed, clearly deeply moved by this sustained effort. 'She must have wanted to be independent in her old age. I know she said quite often she wouldn't stay at Garwood when I married. I always meant to give her an allowance, as much as she wanted. She was so good to me–' His voice faded into broken murmurings.

'You must see Mr Manton, Philip. He admired your mother very much and advised her over her investments. Or some of them. She seems to have been a careful and acute business woman, you know.'

That, Aunt Amy said to herself, astounds me. The last person – but Mr McNee was speaking again.

'There are legacies for Miss Tupper, Mrs Harper and Mr and Mrs Savin. A sum for the Broxbourne church building fund. No other charities favoured. The remainder to my beloved son, Philip.'

'How strange!' The young man was still perplexed by this long-sustained secret hoarding. He had realised as he grew up that they wanted for nothing and any reasonable desires for the house, the estate and his own personal needs had always been met. But all the time she had been saving: no luxuries; no visits abroad, except on his own occasionally to Paris, to the Brittany coast, once to Vienna. Never to Italy. She had never gone abroad herself.

'She was wholly dependent upon your father when she married,' Miss Tupper said, gently. 'Suppose you had died as a child or later, before she did. In either case there would be nothing for her. Those Thorntons would get it all and might not do anything for her.'

'I was about to suggest that motive for her saving,' Mr McNee said, rather stiffly. 'It was a sensible move on her part.'

'I shall give it all away!' Philip declared. 'How can I take it as well as all Garwood?'

'We shall not get probate immediately,' the solicitor told him. 'Wait until you learn the extent of the death duties.'

Two weeks later Miss Tupper had a letter from Philip inviting her to spend the following weekend at Garwood. He had managed to have leave from his school on Friday and would be able to stay until Sunday evening. He had asked a friend to join them and would very much like Aunt Amy to meet her.

So she was now to take up the office of

chaperone, was she, Miss Tupper wondered, laughing to herself. How unusual in these days of sex freedom and sex boasting. Or was the boy afraid of offending dear Harpie and perhaps Irina Savin too? A bunch of girls and boys, quite natural. A solo girl, perhaps a bride on trial, highly undesirable.

Miss Tupper told herself not to be a prurient old fool and sent a postcard with a first-class stamp to accept the invitation.

Philip's guest was a pretty girl, almost as dark as Philip himself and about an inch taller, called Carlotta Moorehead. Her father was English, an electrical engineer consultant, working for a multiple firm in the Midlands and North, with connections in Milan. Her mother was Italian. Carlotta was the youngest of four, having two sisters and one brother. She was nineteen, cheerful and self-confident, but not brash or aggressive, Miss Tupper was thankful to find.

'I've told Irina to put on something special for dinner tonight,' Philip said, as they settled in the shade of trees on the south lawn of the house, waiting for tea to be brought to them by Mandy, the daily assistant to Mrs Harper. 'It's a special occasion, really, in honour of Lotta's prize.'

'Congratulations,' Aunt Amy said. 'What for?'

'The prize? Oral test. I'm doing English and Italian, literature and language. But my mother has always kept up her Italian and we go to see the grandparents quite often. So I think the prize wasn't really fair.'

'Rubbish,' said Philip. 'With fifty per cent of British inhibition over foreign language speaking, inherited from your father, I consider it a great achievement.'

Carlotta made a face at him; Miss Tupper said, 'Really, Pip, that was worthy of a B.B.C interviewer at his worst.'

His indignant denial was lost in the arrival of Mrs Harper with a light garden table, which he sprang up to take from her, and Mandy with the tea tray.

'Stay and have some with us, Harpie,' he pleaded as she began to turn away. 'I have told Lotta you've known me since I was a few months old.'

'Four months,' the housekeeper said smiling, and as Philip ran off to find a chair for her, she added. 'A proper little love then, almost too quiet, his mother thought. But there was reason enough for that.'

Philip came back with a chair for Mrs Harper and Aunt Amy poured the tea, remarking as she did so, 'Harpie has been telling Miss Moorehead–'

'Carlotta,' the girl corrected.

'Lotta,' Philip added.

'Telling us,' Miss Tupper resumed, not accepting correction, 'how wonderful you were as a baby, Pip. The rot set in early, though, didn't it, Harpie?'

'Well,' Mrs Harper smiled lovingly at the 'little master' she had always adored. 'He didn't give his mother or me or anyone else real trouble, except for his venturesome ways. Much too early. Frightened the life out of poor Mrs Bennet the first time she saw him at it.'

'At what, Mrs Harper?' Carlotta asked. She had been getting bored by all this baby worship from the two old dears. Philip – Phil to her, not Pip, certainly not Pip – was a real dish and it was a strange, a bit unnerving, surprise to find he already owned a big house and all that went with it. Cindy set-up, one of her friends had told her, laughing. Well, she was damned if she'd play Cinderella to any orphan Prince. She asked again in a harsh voice, 'What did Phil's mother catch him at, she didn't like?'

'Walking along the top of the boundary wall, it being nine feet up and covered with glass,' Mrs Harper said quietly, sensing the challenge and meeting it with calm truth. 'He was six at the time.'

'Nine foot wall? How did he get up there?'

'Ladder, of course,' said Philip, who had heard this quite ordinary tale far too often. 'Harpie doesn't like heights, never did, so these childish exploits of mine have stuck in her memory. I wouldn't have remembered them at all myself otherwise.'

141

Miss Tupper intervened.

'Except the time when he was ten and walked along the roof parapet to pick up a ball that had been hit up in the air by a friend and lodged in the gutter.'

'Which roof?'

'Over there. Opposite. He said he'd get it and ran into the house before anyone could stop him. He climbed out of the top window, reached up to the gutter, swung himself up to the sloping roof, straightened up, walked along to the ball, reached down for it, threw it down, turned round, walked back, lowered himself to the window-ledge– I didn't see that, because Florence, his mother, had fainted and I was attending to her.'

'He swung on the gutter till he got his feet on the window-ledge,' said Mrs Harper, shuddering a little as she spoke. 'Then he got one hand on to the top of the open window and was inside again in a jiffy.'

'You saw all that?' Carlotta asked, unable to accept it.

'We were watching the children's cricket. From just about here. We didn't say much to him. He saw what he'd done to his mother.'

Carlotta swung round to Philip.

'You actually did all that the way Mrs Harper says you did?'

'I don't ever mind heights,' he said, slightly irritated by this dragging up of old exploits

142

that he had never thought were important. 'And I've always had reasonably good balance.'

The subject was dropped. Conversation languished. Tea was over and Miss Tupper decided to help Mrs Harper to take away the tray and the table and leave the young people to themselves. Besides, she wanted to hear the latest news, for she had not heard anything from the police or from Philip since she was last at Garwood.

But there was little to hear. Mrs Harper and the Savins were very well. Mandy was the younger sister of Gladys, who had been with Florence at the time of her disappearance but had left in disgrace, dismissed by Mr Bennet in his first access of rage. Mrs Harper had seen the girl only once.

'I remember,' Miss Tupper said. 'Of course. You had Mandy instead for a time, then. Gladys never came back at all.'

'Mandy left to be married. A Broxbourne man and she's always willing to oblige again now that her children are grown up, of course. For a half day, now and then. She doesn't really need the money, but she likes to keep up the connection. She's shocked by this dreadful murder, but she isn't frightened off by it, like all the young ones are, or pretend to be.'

Miss Tupper sighed. How was Philip, so young, so inexperienced, going to deal with all that would have to be revalued when the police had done their work and found the killer and laid bare whatever lurked behind the crime.

A totally unexpected revelation more than fulfilled her forebodings. It happened early on Sunday afternoon. Philip with his two guests were drinking their after-lunch coffee in another shady part of the garden, where a rather over-grown shrubbery swallowed up part of the lawn, swelling out over the grass in a straggly heap, chiefly laurel, mixed with untidy branches of rhododendron.

'We ought to have had the tennis court here,' Philip explained to Carlotta. 'Much better for light, and shelter from the wind. But mother wouldn't have it. She had quite a thing about this part of the garden. Boris always says the laurels stifle the rhododendrons and I think that's true, but mother said quite the opposite.'

'I don't remember this at all,' Aunt Amy protested. She would have liked to indulge in a small comfortable nap in this lovely part of the garden, so she murmured encouragingly, 'Why don't you two go off for a quick game of tennis? You'll both be stuck in your cars driving away all the evening.'

'Tennis! God forbid!' Philip said, but asked plaintively, 'You feeling like hitting a ball about in the sun?'

'Like hell I would,' Carlotta answered,

with feeling. 'After walking those miles and miles all morning. Lovely views, of course. But I ask you, *more* bloo– More *exercise?* No, thank you.'

There was silence, which Carlotta broke by asking, 'Why did your mother mind about the tennis court's position, anyway?'

'She was a great gardener,' Philip said. 'Didn't like to be contradicted over garden matters. I don't suppose you understand that. Your people have always lived in towns, haven't they?'

'That's right.'

'Besides,' Philip went on, still defending his mother from alien criticism, though he had started it himself, 'her little animal cemetery is in that tangle. Perhaps she didn't want it disturbed.'

Miss Tupper was amazed.

'Animal cemetery! What on earth do you mean, Pip?'

'When I was about nine, I must have been. I was home for the holidays, exploring round the place because I'd been away at school. The laurels had been my chief hiding place when I wanted to get away alone. Well, I knelt on something hard and it was a kind of tin box. I pulled it out a bit and tried to open it. Ideas of buried treasure and all that.'

He laughed. Carlotta said, 'Go on! what was it, old bottles?'

'It was a skeleton,' Philip said awkwardly.

'At least, I looked in through a corner of the lid I managed to prise up. There was a small round head, a cat's head, I thought. Cat's cemetery. I got a trowel and dug a deeper hole for it and pushed the box in. I didn't like to tell anyone. It was one of my places, as I told you, where I liked to go and hide and they might have stopped me using it. Mother might not have liked her cemetery disturbed.'

'It can't have been her,' said Aunt Amy. 'Florence never had pets of any kind. Are you sure it was near here?'

'I'll show you,' he said. 'Even if it wasn't mother's I might as well prove I'm not pulling your legs, both of you. Perhaps it was my father's when he was a boy, when he might have had a pet.'

He went away and fetched a long fork and spade. It seemed hardly worth the effort, he felt, but having committed himself he set his mind to working out where the present position of that box could be. After an hour or so, casting about and probing, his fork struck metal and he dug up a battered, oblong tin box, fastened securely, but with one end bent and loosened, so that it could be lifted a little.

'There you see!' Philip said triumphantly. 'Small round head, like I told you. Dead pussy, don't you think?'

Carlotta shuddered away, but Aunt Amy,

ever curious, said, 'Open it if you can, Pip.'

When he did so they saw the round skull had a flat face in front with a small jaw, no teeth, a short neck, a straight spine behind with a rib cage and a few broken ribs attached. There were bony parts of four limbs, some lying apart, some attached. Fragments of material grey, mouldy, perhaps wool, perhaps silk, lay over and around the collection of small bones. There was as well a little dirty yellowing bone ring. with two rusty bells still attached to it.

Carlotta said, with a kind of shrinking admiration. 'A favourite cat with its favourite play bells! Pathetic!'

But Miss Tupper, white-faced, pointed to the little five-membered end of one fore-limb and whispered, 'No cat's paw was ever made with those bones. Human bones! A baby's hand! Oh, dear God in heaven, a baby's bones and a baby's favourite toy!'

10

Without waiting to find out if Detective Superintendent Holmes was at the Incident Centre, Philip and Aunt Amy drove there with the tin box and its sad contents wrapped clumsily in brown paper. The untidy appearance of the parcel was due to the intense agitation and bewilderment still afflicting Philip and his friends, including Mrs Harper, who suffered a second overwhelming shock. But this very shortly gave way to anger.

'No!' she declared, over and over again. 'Not in my time! Certainly not! The very idea!'

Miss Tupper, desperately trying to find some explanation that would shield Philip from the blow she foresaw as inevitable, said, 'It would not be in any way a fault of yours – your– But the helps in the house, during the war, after the war – they came and went, didn't they? Still do. So unreliable!' She stopped, miserably staring at the box, remembering the pathetic little remains in their mouldy discoloured wrappings and that all too recognisable ring with the small rusty bells.

Mrs Harper had recovered control now.

'In the whole of my time here,' she declared, 'I have never been aware of any one of my girls being pregnant or making an attempt to hide it. They've left to get married and not before time, I've often wondered, but there's never been anything said, and why should there, these days?'

'I suppose not,' said Miss Tupper, who had lived quite long enough in theatrical circles to lose any wish to carp at or criticise the modern standards accepted at nearly every level of society.

Philip broke into what seemed to him a stupid waste of time.

'We've got to tell the cops about this bloody find, haven't we? I'll run it down to their Centre now. You coming, Aunt Amy?'

It was not until they reached the gates on the lane that he said, 'Where's Carlotta?'

'She went home,' Aunt Amy told him. 'She asked me what she ought to do and said she was upset and felt sick. I said she'd better rest and that you would have to see the police about the skeleton and she said she'd better go. To London, is it?'

'Yes.'

'Didn't you know she'd gone?'

'I noticed her car wasn't where she'd parked it.'

'So?'

'Nothing.'

He did not speak again until they reached

the Incident Centre and were relieved to find Detective Superintendent Holmes was there and willing to see them at once.

The superintendent took their unexpected news with less than enthusiasm. It was curious, of course, perhaps interesting, in a professional way, to be able to date the thing at least as far back as fourteen years, when young Bennet as a child had unearthed it and put it back in the ground.

But the lab. would have to date it more accurately. A boy of nine could not be blamed for mistaking it for a dead cat or some other pet with a roundish skull and a flattish, forward-looking face. The position of the box and the shallowness of the grave did suggest a pets' cemetery.

'Why didn't you tell your mother about it?' he asked Philip.

The young man considered.

'I think I didn't want to upset her by prising up the lid a bit. Unseemly curiosity, morbid, rather nasty. And embarrassing, too. I was an only child, of course. I don't think I ever wanted to share my feelings with anyone.'

Miss Tupper nodded.

'Florence always said you were a very reserved little boy.'

Detective Superintendent Holmes had had enough of this, to him, totally irrelevant material.

'You were right to turn it in,' he told Philip. 'I shall have to have it vetted for timing, if possible, medical findings, ditto, fact of undeclared human death, or possibly still-birth.'

'Nothing more I ought to do?' Philip asked.

'No, sir. You had a duty to declare this find, but clearly no further responsibility.'

Miss Tupper said nothing and they drove back to Garwood in a heavy silence. Philip's morose withdrawal was due to Carlotta's sudden flight without warning, without saying goodbye to him. This the old lady guessed and was further distressed by it.

Later that day when Philip was again in the shrubbery with Boris Savin, discussing an alteration to the whole of it that would obliterate in time the memory of its unhappy secret and late exposure, Miss Tupper rang up the detective again to ask for, as very urgent, another interview.

Most reluctantly, Holmes agreed. He had no wish to see her again. But she was the only witness in this case, if you could call her that, who had given him any positive information. She said she had some more and she wanted it to be kept absolutely secret at present. This smacked of melodrama, as did her proposal to meet him in the lane and be driven by him to the Centre, instead of getting there in her own car.

152

'A good thing I didn't ask Savin to get Mrs Bennet's car out,' she said as they drove off. 'He's the gardener as well and Philip is with him now at the bottom of the lawn, where we found the box.'

Holmes said nothing, until he had his heavily co-operative informer sitting opposite him in his own office.

'The bone ring and its bells with the baby's skeleton,' said Aunt Amy slowly, 'belonged to Florence's baby, Philip, and he would never be parted from it. I saw the ring in his tiny fist several times when I visited. Three months old. Four months. But never later.'

'How much later?'

'Never after her absence, her breakdown, whatever happened to her, to them both; never after she was back here.'

'But you recognise the bone ring? You are quite sure it is the one the baby always wanted to hold?'

'I am certain of it. And the bones are her real baby's bones. And Pip is not— Oh, my God, who is Pip? Poor Pip!'

Miss Tupper burst into tears, rocking herself to and fro and sobbing aloud.

Detective Superintendent Holmes ordered tea and the policewoman who had sat in on the interview, astonished and delighted by the developing drama, decided that she might try for promotion on the intelligence side.

Holmes left the room when the tea arrived. Miss Tupper had come up with a nugget of pure gold this time, if true, and could be proved true. That rumour in the village, thought to be started by old Mrs Somerton and somehow persisting against all reason, might be correct after all. If young Mr Bennet was not the original Philip, then who the hell was he, and where did he come from? But before all that it must be proved he was not old Percy's child.

Holmes sent for Detective Sergeant Tom Miles. He gave him this new development.

'I shall take it up at once with the doctor,' he said. 'Even before the lab. tells us what they think of the bones. Don't know why I didn't go into this line before, except there seemed no point.'

'What line, sir?' Miles had lost the thread.

'Blood groups, of course. We hear enough of them in paternity cases, don't we?'

'Yes, of course. But the old man's dead.'

'O.K. Car crash. With luck not dead when found. Blood group taken. Might carry the group symbol about with him. Many do. Never mind. I'll take all that up with Dr Armstrong. All happened in his old partner's time, but they have good records in that practice. You carry on with the Weymouth garage. Any joy there?'

'Not so far, sir. But there's one, the owner, seems to be known by us in connection with

154

Customs. In trouble himself and turned informer to get out of it. I'm still going through records. Bennet or Atkins, isn't it?'

'That's right.'

Dr Armstrong was not altogether surprised to see Detective Superintendent Holmes. The detective chose to visit the doctor at his own house, because he knew how touchy the medical profession was over disclosing information about their patients, dead or alive. So he asked for an interview away from the police atmosphere of the Incident Centre with its listening and recording facilities.

When he described the strange, pitiful discovery at Garwood, Philip's story of his childhood's mistake, and the village's uneasy suspicions, always denied and often ridiculed, the doctor interrupted brusquely.

'Of course I know that old wives' tale,' he exclaimed, 'though I didn't inherit the practice for years after old Bennet was killed.'

'But you kept the old records, I hope, sir?'

'Naturally. In fact when this present dreadful business happened I looked up Percy's old notes, ending with his death. And Philip's too.'

'With blood groups?'

Dr Armstrong stared at him.

'So *that's* why you're here,' he said, slowly. 'Well now, I've got young Philip's. He cut his right calf rather badly, slipping on top of a high wall he was walking along. Always at these acrobatic tricks, young Philip, showing off, served him right. He was on holiday from his prep school. Half a mo. I've got it handy.'

He pulled out a drawer in his desk to bring out a folder. Holmes saw it was not a N.H.S. folder but clearly one for the private part of the doctor's practice.

'Here we are. Yes. We ran him in to our local cottage hospital, still running in the 'fifties, closed now, of course. Dr Shore wanted the boy to have tetanus injections, which we had not got here. We did our own minor surgery at the hospital, at least Dr Shore had an F.R.C.S. so he was used to doing anything up to and including appendisectomy: I gave the anaesthetics.'

'So you needed the blood group?'

'I have it here.'

'And Mr Percy's?'

Dr Armstrong shook his head.

'Not in our notes. Practically nothing in our notes. I certainly never saw him professionally. But he was taken to Dorchester after his crash, not straight to the public mortuary. Must have been still alive. They may have it.'

'What about the baby?'

'Philip? I've just told—'

'The infant Philip. Do you know where he

was born?'

'Ah. Yes. Maternity home. Nothing in his notes about anything before two years, three months, rash, German measles.'

Dr Armstrong laughed. Detective Superintendent Holmes looked grave.

'So typical,' Dr Armstrong said apologetically. 'A rash that goes very quickly, does not make the patient ill and is only dangerous, but *very* dangerous, if any contact is in the early months of pregnancy. The boy was over two, his mother a widow, the Garwood living-in staff middle-aged.'

Holmes ignored all this and said, 'Well, thank you, doctor, for the information. I must ask you not to divulge any of our conversation to anyone, please sir.'

'As if I would! Poor young Philip! What a cruel blow if it works out the way you want. What an appalling thing!'

'I neither want it nor don't want it,' Holmes said. 'I want the truth and I want the man who murdered Mrs Bennet.'

The police records that Detective Sergeant Tom Miles sifted from the old records relating to Customs and Excise operations were meagre. A Weymouth garage owner called Pullen, struggling to set himself up in the years just after the Second World War, had sailed too near the wind on several occasions. He was suspected of harbouring

157

smuggled goods from the Continent for days on end. Until, in fact, the heat was off, if it had ever been there, and they could be split up and distributed to their various buyers in this country. After one or two tip-offs and consequent searches of the garage, with no outright success for the police and no real evidence and with a certain amount of sympathy for a youngish man trying to promote a reasonable living for himself and his family, a far-seeing chief superintendent had visited Joe Pullen with a proposal. His ploy would be brought to court with insufficient evidence, so the charge would not stick. But he would be blown as far as his regular customers were concerned. In return he would, in future, inform the police of suspicious actions by anyone using his garage, with or without his personal knowledge, for any suspicious purpose. He would be paid for this work.

Pullen, who saw clearly that the former game was up for him at least, accepted the new conditions. The cops, if he refused, would work all out to get that evidence they lacked so far. He would go in fear meanwhile, reluctant to accept any more illicit parcels for temporary storage, afraid to refuse for fear of reprisals.

The open court case should be enough to warn off the smugglers, he was told. They would blame the Law, not himself, for upsetting their system. They would soon arrange another: an added risk to them, unless he was stupid enough to disclose his change of allegiance.

Joe saw the point and though the police pay was far less than his former gain, he did pretty well out of it. The cunning determination and occasional recklessness that had preserved him before, came to his aid in his new role. His reports came in quite frequently. Sometimes they were useful at once, more often they helped in the long run. Occasionally, as in the case of Miss Maisie Atkins, they led nowhere. Until Detective Sergeant Miles took the report to his superior.

'The name's different, sir,' he explained apologetically, 'but finding that pram, cot, and such–'

'The name's right,' said Holmes. 'Mrs B. was an actress before she married. Maisie Atkins was her stage name, I've been waiting for this. No baby, but cot and pram in boot. Car number same as Grant the chauffeur gave me. Left on packet for St Malo. Two suitcases, no initials on either. Newish-looking cases. Blue.'

'Second report gives return of Maisie Atkins six days later. Had paid in advance for two weeks' garaging. Not asked for more, nor given return change for a week. No wedding ring.' Sergeant Miles looked up. 'She'd been wearing a ring to begin with when she left the car, but had slipped it off when she handed over the money. Pullen notes this at the end of the second report, adding that she had no ring on when she took the car away.'

Detective Superintendent Holmes leaned back in his chair.

'Thorough, isn't he?' he said. 'So she went to France for those six days without a baby. Pullen thinks it was to do with smuggling, or could be. A smuggled baby, perhaps, if that miserable scrap in the tin box was hers, not some by-blow dumped in Garwood shrubbery.'

'She had a nerve, sir, hadn't she?'

'Like hell, she did. No further reports on Miss Atkins?'

'Hardly any further reports at all, sir. Mr Pullen seems to have dried up from then on.'

The two men exchanged glances. Their thoughts were running parallel.

'Another source of perks?' suggested Holmes. 'The news of Percy Bennet's death and Mrs B.'s disappearance were widely spread by the media. I've checked that. Pullen could draw conclusions. Go through those again, Tom. Local papers specially. Did any of them mention Mrs B.'s other name? If so he'd jump at it when she turned up again. Why didn't he? Any report to us?'

160

'Blackmail,' said Miles. 'Better pay there.'

'Too right,' said Holmes. 'Go after Pullen, Tom. Must be getting on now. In his sixties. Habits. Visits. Get a photo. Try it on Bert Elbury at the pub here for any visits recently.'

'Sir.'

Left to himself, Holmes turned his thoughts back to the problem of Philip Bennet's identity. It seemed more likely than ever that he had, in fact, been a replacement for the original baby Philip. If so, the village rumour would be satisfied, but there was still no clue to his origin.

But it might explain much of Mrs Bennet's behaviour over the years of her supposed son's childhood, until his coming of age. Her careful saving from the large family income in small amounts collected in her own name. Had she foreseen or at least feared an ultimate disclosure? She had amassed a quite sizeable capital, well invested. Philip, the present one, poor lad, would not be destitute if he had to give up his so-called inheritance to the real heirs, who had been pressing for it, Mr McNee had told him, since old Percy died.

Again, Mrs Bennet, if blackmailed steadily for over twenty years, must have realised, when Philip gained control of the Garwood estate and all monies connected with it, that she could no longer make savings from it. It was in Philip's control. Perhaps she expected him to make her an allowance. They were a close and affectionate pair, he understood. Probably she had told him she had saved to provide for herself. It was partly true, of course. She had expected and hoped he would marry and have children.

But the change in control gave her a prime excuse for refusing to pay any further blackmail. Made it impossible for her to do so without destroying her careful nest-egg.

So had the blackmailer lost his temper and struck out? Too hard? Destroying the source? Unlikely. But possible. Wait for young Miles to report. The chief constable was beefing again. He'd better explain to him the reports on Pullen and the garage. Nothing of substance, except that they knew, if they accepted Pullen's doubtful word, that Mrs Bennet, as Maisie Atkins, had embarked at Weymouth, without her baby, and come back, method of transport unknown, to Pullen's garage, to retrieve her car, still apparently childless.

The chief constable found this news meagre, but understood the difficulties.

162

11

Detective Sergeant Miles had no difficulty in proving that Bert Elbury's visiting stranger was the man the police knew as an occasional informer in the Customs line of their business.

His usefulness to the Law had been infrequent, growing more and more rare as the years went by. After all, he had his garage business, which, on the outskirts of a thriving sea-side town, could not fail to prosper under any reasonable management. Mr Pullen was an eminently reasonable man; must be so, Miles decided, to avoid real trouble when he switched his allegiance to the Law from masters not usually complaisant under betrayal. But Mr Pullen had prospered. His garage was fitted with all the modern conveniences, self-wash, instant M.O.T. overhaul, brisk girls at the pumps in attractive uniforms; strong girls and hefty mechanics, several of them, Miles counted. No one was going to jump Mr Pullen in the office; a lean man, looking younger than fifty-eight, which must be his age if the police records were correct.

He showed no surprise when Tom Miles

announced himself. Only said, 'What's this about?'

'It's about the murder of Mrs Bennet of Garwood House three days ago. I think you knew her.'

Mr Pullen shook his head.

'You knew her over twenty years ago as Miss Maisie Atkins. You put in a report on her as a suspect smuggler, query drugs, query watches or such.'

'Well, I'll be damned!' The surprise in the voice was markedly artificial. 'Was that her real name? Well, I'm blowed! You never told me.'

'Come off it!' Detective Sergeant Miles was not going to be played with. 'Don't tell me, after she came back to you for her car, with that baby gear in the boot, that you'd seen already, you didn't connect her with the search of the last three days before that for the missing wife and child of Mr Percy Bennet? Not that you put that idea in your second report to us.'

'I wondered,' Pullen agreed. 'But I forgot it later. Nothing to do with me.'

'O.K. So how come you drive over to Broxbourne now and then to see the lady? Keep up the connection, eh?'

Mr Pullen looked at him pityingly.

'I drive all over this country, lad,' he said, leaning back to look Miles full in the face. 'I've stopped at a-many pubs, too. But I can honestly say I've never driven up to Garwood House, though I do know its whereabouts.'

'Walked up from the road as a rule, did you? The housekeeper says you came by car. Lateish. The night she was killed.'

Mr Pullen lost his temper quite suddenly. He brought his palms smacking down on his desk, at the same time hoisting himself to his feet. He lifted a closed fist as Miles stepped back, but it was only to fling the arm out towards the door. Speech was choked, the detective saw, and moved away quickly, with Pullen behind him.

On the busy forecourt Miles saw the mechanics turn, freeze, lift expectant eyebrows. A mechanic in the workshop doorway lifted an outsize spanner from the blackened grease where a van had stood. Miles saw the awareness, the eager anticipation, fade, and without turning, understood. Pullen had refused help or any kind of action.

Which was all to the good, for the place was empty of customers just then and of cars, except his own.

It gave no trouble in starting, nor did it stop or blow up or in any way let him down as he drove back to report to Detective Superintendent Holmes.

'Denies knowing Mrs Bennet, sir. Lost his cool when I tried to press him and threw me out. But I've got a nice picture, I think. At least, I hope it is.'

He unfastened the tiny camera he had employed when Pullen had leaned back to look up at him.

'Shouldn't wonder if he knew that was what I was there for,' he said. 'He's got quite an ugly lot working for him, boys *and* girls. Shouldn't like to tangle with any of them.'

'O.K.,' Holmes said. It sounded as if young Miles had been less than tactful, but that might do no harm. Pullen was no sensitive flower, far from it. He might well confess to a spot of blackmail as cover for some more deadly crime. But kill the goose–? Most unlikely.

The photograph, blown up to reasonable size, was recognised at once by Bert Elbury. Mrs Harper thought she had seen the gentleman, but could not recollect where, exactly. Or when.

The days passed. It was now mid-summer and Broxbourne was enjoying a warm dry spell after much rain had held back the summer flowers, reducing the rosebuds to sodden, brown-tipped lumps, disclosing fat slugs among the dahlia shoots, and other discouragements to keen gardeners.

Now, unexpectedly, all was changed. In a week the glories of June shone behind every hedge and the usual ungrateful comments began to be heard, with hints of drought

166

coming, the labour of watering, the dangers of forest fires.

Not that Broxbourne was likely to suffer from such, as there were neither forests nor commons in its immediate neighbourhood. On the contrary most of the keen gardeners in the village, and there were many among the retired, pensioned, inhabitants, were very thankful to be able to burn up their garden rubbish at last, while the compost had a chance to settle and develop.

Philip was home for the half-term holiday. Though he was the youngest of the three junior masters, his Head was anxious to avoid any fresh publicity that might grow from parents meeting him when they arrived to take away their boys. He would be better out of sight. It was not the poor boy's fault his mother had been murdered. All the same, for any woman to attract that sort of attention she must have made some undesirable contacts in her life. Or, allowing for modern violence on the part of unknown burglars, an extraordinary lack of the correct protection for her house.

So Philip was back at Garwood, with three friends he had invited to join him: a former school buddy, with his young wife, and a college friend, equally interested in games and particularly in athletics.

They spent two days of the long weekend at the sea and the third in the garden at

Garwood, mostly sun-bathing, occasionally playing a little lazy tennis, before cooling off in the shade of trees and complaining about the continual smoke from village fires that blew across them whenever a breeze got up, as it did so often in mid-afternoon, during the fine weather.

Carlotta was not of the party. Philip had understood and respected her revulsion over the exhumation of the baby. He had hoped to explain it to her but neither the police nor Dr Armstrong had told him anything, except that it was being examined at the police laboratory. In the meantime it must on no account get into the papers, nor should he discuss it with anyone at all, however unconnected with Garwood, Broxbourne, or anywhere else.

All the same he had hoped she would at least write. They had exchanged letters fairly frequently. She was by no means his first girl-friend but she had been rather special, so far. He had felt more discomfort, to be honest, real pain, in her defection than ever before. Oh well, live and learn. And it had been a nasty moment in the garden when Aunt Amy had produced that old teething ring.

Just the sort of thing a pet pussy might have had. Surely it was time he heard from the lab.

While he had enjoyed the company of his

friends very much indeed at the beginning of the half-term weekend, Philip thought more and more about Carlotta as the prospect of its ending drew closer. A quiet day in the sunny garden, with no exercise of any kind to speak of, except that feeble game of tennis, did not help. He was in a restless mood when the others drifted off to bed, did himself no good by reading the whole of a particularly gory thriller before following them and lay awake wanting Carlotta and cursing the smoke-laden air that had plagued them off and on all day.

Smoke. He must have dozed. He flung himself over to his other side, pushing away the sheet, his only covering for that summer night.

Smoke!

He sat up, coughing, his eyes beginning to smart. He jumped to the wide-open window and hung over the sill. Smoke was pouring from somewhere below and there was crackling and almost at once a red glow on the smoke.

Philip was out of his room in a second, dashing to the floor below where his visitors were sleeping in two rooms with windows overlooking the side and back of the house. He roused them with shouts and orders that dragged them awake, stupid with sleep, but not incapable of understanding.

'Fire! Can't you hear, you clots! Fire! Out!

Take your things! Front door! Out!'

He left them, all three scrabbling and swearing, but moving. There was very little smoke in their rooms and none he found, thankfully, as he leaped on his way.

Reverting to childhood he slid down banisters, flung his legs over them at the bend near the bottom and dropped neatly to the hall near the telephone there. When he dialled 999 and called 'Fire! Garwood House, Broxbourne!' an answering voice said, 'Garwood House, Broxbourne. Fire already reported. Engine on its way.'

Who on earth? Philip thought wildly, but did not stop moving as he pulled back the chains at the top and bottom of the front door, pulled back the lock and opened it.

Smoke poured in, but no flames. The crackling now grew louder though, and when he dashed out on to the drive he saw that the blaze was at the far end of the house front, inside the office room and as he stopped aghast, he saw the window bulge and break and the flames spring out and roar upwards.

He dashed back and up the stairs. His friends were just staggering from their rooms. They had pulled on slacks and vests and sandals and were carrying bundles.

'Get on outside, quick!' he yelled at them, already up on the next flight of the stairs.

'Come on yourself,' one of them shouted

back, pausing as the others obeyed the order. 'What in hell–?'

'Harpie!' Philip shouted back, but saved his breath from explaining further.

She was up, poor woman, huddled into a coat over her nightdress, standing at the door of her bedroom, too confused and frightened to move further.

'Oh, Mr Pip!' she said, 'What is it? Not *fire?* Not–'

'Yes, Harpie. Fire in the office. Not much yet. They're on their way. Be here any minute now.'

He stretched a hand to her, which she seized eagerly and held tightly as he led her carefully down the stairs to the next landing.

'No, not your stairs,' he said, as they reached it.

Useless to try the back staircase: the lower and ground floors would be impassable now. He paused outside his own room. The smoke was increasing second by second. They were both coughing, their eyes blinded as they filled. Harpie would never make it to the hall even though the flames had not yet got anywhere near the main part of the house.

He pulled her into his bedroom and to the window, where he propped her up with her head and shoulders outside. Though the smoke swept over them in choking gusts there was fresh air between. And as they hung there, alternately gasping and holding their breath, while below on the lawn beyond the drive and the terrace a growing crowd gathered, suddenly a cheer rose from them and the fire engine, the crew hanging on with one hand and fixing their helmets with the other, drove up and stopped with a jerk.

Very promptly the watchers pointed to the two figures at the third-floor window, Philip waving his pocket torch and his bright yellow bath towel. While some of the men ran out hoses, directed to a hydrant by Boris Savin, who had appeared five minutes before, another pair operated the ladder.

It rose, it appeared to the two at the window, who hailed it with cries of joy; it stopped. The fireman ran up to the top and shouted. Philip shouted back, then turned to Mrs Harper.

But she had understood already. She was moaning, 'They can't reach us! Oh, God have mercy! Oh, Lord!'

'Not to worry,' Philip told her, though he was desperate at this setback. He yelled down, 'I'll lower her. Hang on!'

He knotted his sheets together and added the thin silk bed-cover. He tied one end round Mrs Harper's waist and looped the other round the leg of the bed nearest to the window. He pushed the bed closer.

'I'm going to lower you to him,' he said. 'You'll be all right. Come on, Harpie. Hop up on the bed and put a leg out. I'll help you, but you've got to do your bit to help me. You always have, you know.'

She was on the verge of collapse, but this familiar appeal roused her.

'You and your tricks,' she said valiantly and tucking up her nightdress, regardless of propriety, she scrambled up until she sat across the window sill, holding on tightly to the window frame.

'Let go!' yelled Philip and the fireman together. She still held on, but a fresh wave of smoke engulfed her and coughing she collapsed forward, Philip straining to control her untidy descent to the fireman. But the man was used to these bundles falling from the sky; he caught her neatly and was about to untie the sheet rope from her middle when Philip who had untied it from the bed, dropped it down to him.

'Bloody idiot!' the fireman shouted. 'How'll I get you down now?'

'Can't stay here,' Philip shouted back. 'Too much frigging smoke! Look out for me over the front door. Take her down, you fool! I'm all right!'

The fireman, deciding the man was mad and feeling Mrs Harper's sagging weight needed his full attention, disappeared into the smoke.

Philip did not wait. Though the fire was not spreading, for the hoses were hissing away now, the smoke was, if anything, getting thicker. He must be able to see his way by the route he would take.

It was not new to him, though he had not used it for a year or two. He had developed it during his school days, adding routes to those he had first developed, including that walk along the gutter that had so much upset his poor mother when he was quite a young child. He ran quickly up to Harpie's room and across it to the window.

He left this window, a dormer one, drew himself upright and moved carefully up the side of it and on up the tiles to the complex of chimneys that served that end of the house and the kitchen premises. From there he set off along the topmost ridge of the roof. It was a narrow pathway indeed, but for long now he had not dared to use the gutter. He was far too heavy for it and the fall was some forty feet. That in his present position he was over sixty feet from the ground did not trouble him. As he kept telling people, who did not believe him, he never had minded heights.

But he did mind his present walk along the six-inch track, for sometimes he could see his way and sometimes the smoke swirled across and he was walking in a fog, so thick he could see nothing ahead. No good to stop anyhow. To stop was to sway, perhaps, and to sway was to fall. So he went on, from memory really, and he almost sobbed his joy when the opposite chimney stack came up before him, so suddenly, but so comfortingly, that he put his arms round it in affectionate relief, only to snatch them back, for the bricks were burning hot and both arms and hands were scorched. The chimney must be on fire inside: the whole house must be ablaze.

He climbed on, however, down to the balcony over the main porch, down to the porch itself, burning his hands again, sometimes, also his bare feet. Once, when he slipped and sat down on the lower tiles, the heat to his bottom made him spring up and nearly topple over.

But at the porch itself, as he stood up straight at last, he heard a welcoming cheer and a voice through a megaphone bellowed, 'Stand still! We'll be with you in half a jiffy!'

They had to lift him down the short ladder to the ground and the ambulance men who had already loaded up Mrs Harper took one look at him and put him inside as well. His friends, who had run forward to greet him with praise and relief, were swept aside as he was rushed away.

The damage to Garwood was less than everyone had feared. But who had put in that first call to the Fire Brigade? The police could not find out. No one confessed to making the call. So arson or a shy observer? But why not rouse the household, rather than give the call? Much more likely to be arson. More than likely, in mid-summer, however dry outdoors. Though no evidence of arson, at least in a first search for it. And a grand story for the Press. Who had a grudge against the Bennet family? The old lady knocked off and the son likely to have been the same, only he turned out such a first-class acrobat.

'Best bit of circus I've seen these many years,' the fire chief said, describing Philip's escape along the roof of the burning house.

At the prep school Philip's Headmaster shook his head sadly. Young Bennet would miss school again, for weeks probably, most of the rest of the summer term, when he was expected to be more useful than at any other time of year. He had already missed the sports. How fortunate that he was so well provided for, even if the ancestral home *was* badly damaged.

With his second-in-command to help him, the Headmaster composed an advertisement for a junior master, able to teach at middle school level and able to coach in gym and games.

12

Philip stayed in hospital for a week. Not on account of his injuries, though the burns were painful and a full recovery from them could be expected more certainly if the treatment was fully up to date, as Dr Armstrong was only too eager to agree.

There were other reasons. First, he could not go back to teaching at his school with both arms out of action except for a limited extent at meal times. Secondly, in his disabled state he would be worse than useless at home. Garwood House had suffered rather more from drowning than burning. The Fire Brigade had soused the whole interior very thoroughly, and though they had saved the roof and most of the outer fabric, the furniture, carpets, pictures and ornaments, the lighting and all the kitchen equipment had suffered very severely.

Mrs Harper had recovered quickly from her ordeal. In fact, once she knew her young master was safe and not seriously damaged, she gave far less evidence of shock than he did. They kept her in hospital for twenty-four hours, after which the Savins came for her in Philip's car and took her to their flat above the Garwood garage, from where she intended to mobilise her dailies and start to restore the house to its former state of excellence. Or at least that part of it capable of immediate recovery.

But she found two major obstacles in her way. The first was the police, with the insurance assessors, investigating the cause of the fire. They allowed her to go into the relatively unaffected part of the house, but denied her all access to her own room, the floor below it or the corridors and back stairs leading to that part of the house.

The second obstacle was the media, in multiple form, local and national, with photographers and recorders, a television van in the offing, all trying to rush police guards to get at her, to extract the dramatic personal story of her rescue and the young man's escape over the roof.

'Wanting to know my feelings all along,' Mrs Harper said. 'As if I had time for feelings. Me and Mr Pip were too busy saving our skins for any nonsense of that sort. Fright. Yes. Till he ran up my stairs. Not after.'

'But the smoke? The flames? Choking? Terrifying?' they said.

'Young man,' she said, 'haven't you ever made a garden fire of rubbish and that, and never learned how to breathe through it? Town lad, of course. Ignorant.'

Mrs Harper tried her best to avoid the silly young men, but soon saw she could not hide from them entirely and indeed she was quite pleased in the end to explain how her much-loved Mr Pip had saved her. She took the reporters to the end of the lawn, a chair was brought for her and she had the time of her life, as Detective Superintendent Holmes put it later, giving them the full treatment, including what the papers printed as 'Philip Bennet's death walk, sixty feet up, along the knife-edge of the roof.'

All of which, when he read it in his chair on the balcony outside his hospital ward, made Philip chuckle and brought him surprised admiration from the nurses and junior hospital doctors. It also brought him, to his delighted astonishment, Carlotta Moorehead in person, cool, restrained, solicitous, until the nurse brought her to him and retired tactfully into the ward. After that Carlotta crouched beside his chair, murmuring feeble excuses for her apparent defection, and horror at his injuries.

As Philip was incapable of offering any form of suitable caress in absolution, he simply grinned at her and said there was nothing much the matter with him and he would be going home as soon as Harpie had fixed another room for him and got a bit straight herself.

'She wasn't hurt at all?' Carlotta asked.

'No. Right as rain. The others got out quick as soon as we knew the fire was actually ours, not a blow-up of the ones in the neighbourhood. Harpie and I were the only people in the house when it really got going.' He paused, looking down at her with a happy smile. 'Thank God you weren't there, too. Adding to the hazards.'

'Well, if that's all–' Carlotta, deeply offended, began to scramble to her feet, but at that moment the nurse, who had watched the balcony scene with interest, brought out a small upright chair for the girl, who could only subside on to it, fuming, but speechless.

'Hard luck, darling,' Philip said. But he saw the tears gather in the beautiful eyes still hopelessly fixed upon him, and regardless of the stiffly bandaged arms managed to pull her close and kiss her long and fondly. Then, overcome by all this basic masculine triumph, shared and condoned by Carlotta herself, they both sank into commonplace, cheerfully pointless chat.

Miss Tupper read the newspaper accounts of the fire with horror and indignation, but little surprise. Whoever had such a sense of injury, of grievance, of hatred towards the apparently mild, rather dull Florence Bennet, that her death was the only possible redress, must naturally remain unsatisfied.

For that death had no material consequence except the poor woman's permanent removal from the scene. So more destruction was necessary, was compulsory. Why? In God's name, why? And by whom? Miss Tupper, realising what the confusion at Garwood must be, decided not to offer to go there. For what possible help could she give?

So she wrote to Philip in hospital. She wrote to Mrs Harper at the house. She wrote to Irina Savin to congratulate her and Boris on their prompt calling of the Fire Brigade and continued loyal help.

For this was how the media had accounted for the first call to the Brigade, though it was not the truth. The police had still not traced the call. The Savins had woken late, but done their best subsequently.

Two days later Miss Tupper had a letter from Dr Armstrong that sent her straightaway to Dorset, to meet the doctor and Detective Superintendent Holmes at the police headquarters of the county.

There were others beside these two in the room to which she was taken. A pathologist and a chemist from the police laboratory were introduced to her by Dr Armstrong, who knew them both personally. She was greeted, too, by the Bennet family solicitor, Bruce McNee. Her heart sank, for she recognised at once the significance of his presence, though still doubtful about the demand for her own.

At a word from Holmes Dr Armstrong turned to Miss Tupper, whom he had seated beside him at the table round which they had all gathered as soon as introductions had been made. He began to speak smoothly, kindly, professionally. Almost he concealed the appalling content of his words.

'Miss Tupper, as the only surviving great and continuing friend of the late Florence Bennet and the only person who has given any real assistance to the Law over this difficult and dreadful murder, a totally unexpected result has come to light that would seem to be due to be revealed to you – in the hope–'

'Oh stop! Please *stop!*' Miss Tupper broke in. The earnest kind voice, used to delivering bad news of the ordinary sort, was struggling to express something altogether unusual, terrible, but clearly now proved by all these grave personages. And she could not stand it.

'Forgive me,' she went on. 'You are trying to tell me Pip is not Pip, Philip Bennet. Never could have been. Poor Maisie! Poor wicked, deceitful – all these years–!'

She looked round the table. All these clever, closed faces, regarding her now with interest, perhaps with compassion, a certain curiosity.

'I called her Maisie. That's how I first knew her.'

She paused. When no one spoke she appealed to Detective Superintendent Holmes.

'I'm right, aren't I? That baby's skull? How did you prove–?'

Holmes said simply, 'Yes. Yes, you are right, Miss Tupper. The main fact about Mr Philip Bennet is this. He cannot be the son of Mr Percy Bennet. Mr Percy's blood group was found at the hospital to which he was taken, still living, but unconscious, after his accident. Mr Philip's blood group was known at the cottage hospital when Dr Armstrong's senior partner, Dr Shore, took him for a tetanus injection and treatment for cuts in childhood. Mrs Bennet had her baby in a maternity hospital and the blood groups of both the baby and mother were recorded there. All these records were produced for us. The result is what I said. Young Philip's group is different from Mr Percy's: the baby's agrees with Mr Percy's, though that does not prove paternity in a positive sense. It does prove that the Philip we know is not Mr Percy's son.'

The pathologist said, 'The bones discovered in the garden of Garwood had suffered from being dug up and glimpsed through the half-opened lid, when Philip Bennet, now twenty-two, was about nine, according to him. But they are modern bones, they are those of a very young child, mostly cartilage, a child of a few months old only.'

'I noticed that,' Miss Tupper said, surprisingly. 'That hole in the front of the baby's head, that closes after a year doesn't it? That was open.'

'Quite so.'

'You are observant,' Dr Armstrong said, vaguely disgruntled by the old lady's jumping the gun the way she had.

The specialist chemist said, 'The coverings of the bones were pieces of a small hand-knitted so-called woollen shawl of a composition belonging to the period of the first ten years after the Second World War. Similarly, traces of an artificial silk fabric that had been arranged to line the box. The so-called bone ring and bells were of the kind called teething ring, a type of toy. Again made of substitute post-war materials. A popular, cheap copy of the better class teething ring made of real ivory, with silver bells, often given as christening presents in Victorian times and handed down in well-off families.'

'But not by misers like Percy,' said Aunt Amy bitterly.

Her remark was disregarded. There was silence for a time. Then Holmes said, 'You have not shown much surprise over these

184

revelations, Miss Tupper. Do you swear you had no previous knowledge of them?'

'Of course I do.' She was indignant.

'Never at any time suspected the original baby had died and been replaced?'

'Of course not.'

'Never considered the rumour in the village might be true?'

'No. Never heard of it at all for years.'

Mr McNee intervened.

'You called Mrs Bennet wicked and deceitful just now. What exactly did you mean by that, Miss Tupper?'

'That she was often untruthful, always out to win an advantage on her own behalf, but easily frightened.'

'Do you think, knowing her, that she may have got rid of the baby and absconded?'

'Killed it?' Miss Tupper was aghast. 'Oh, no, not that! Maisie, I mean Florence, was terrified of blood, illness, death, anything of the sort. Ask Mrs Harper how she was nearly hysterical whenever Pip hurt himself.'

Dr Armstrong murmured, 'There is such a thing, well known, as cot death. Her behaviour in not declaring the death, not appealing to Dr Shore for help and advice, bundling the body into the ground and going off by herself agrees with that possibility, I think. She would be terrified of giving the news to Mr Bennet.'

This idea was received in silence, but not

with disagreement. Miss Tupper nodded and turned to Mr McNee.

'You wanted me to be told all this before it was broken to Philip, I suppose?'

'Chiefly, yes,' he answered. 'The knowledge of his real position will be a serious, a devastating blow to him. Without the estate–'

'But not, surely without the legacy from his – from Florence–'

'It came from the estate. She had no other source of income. The Thorntons must inherit, with a twenty-two-year delay.'

The scientists and Dr Armstrong intervened. They had no wish to share in a legal wrangle of such a hopelessly unequal kind.

'The point is,' the doctor insisted, 'young Philip has to be told. He is not Percy Bennet's son. Mrs Bennet was not his mother. We do not know where she found him, who were his real parents. He will have to be told all this and I very much hope, Miss Tupper, you can see your way to staying at Garwood, where he is due back from the hospital tomorrow morning. We three,' he indicated the lawyer and the policeman, 'will come there in the afternoon to break it to him.'

'And point out that we have several valid motives now for his supposed mother's murder,' Holmes said, impatiently. 'That rumour had substance, hadn't it? Something positive, some grievance somewhere, some wish for revenge, or at least for exposure. A very finite wrong in that substitution, not only the wrongful concealment of a death.'

So Aunt Amy called at Garwood, persuaded Mrs Harper that it would be a good thing if she stayed for a day or two to be with Pip when he first saw the damage and the confusion in his home. She got the housekeeper's willing agreement. She had rather expected her recall might be prolonged and had brought a small suitcase with her. She agreed with Mrs Harper that her presence should be a surprise.

The two old women had supper together on trays, watching television.

Philip was stunned. At first, totally unbelieving, he said it was the sort of melodramatic tale that simply did not happen in this day and age: it was a story of mid-Victorian fiction: it could not be true. But the evidence was explained to him: he had to accept it. For already Mr McNee had begun to explain the consequences. Mr Holmes had asked him to do so, the lawyer said, since he had not himself been able to get away to Garwood that day. He would call later. A major fraud had been revealed, though the perpetrator was dead and he, Philip, could not possibly be considered culpable. Indeed, the most terrible wrong had been done him, when he was utterly incapable, entirely helpless, at a few months old, of having any part whatever in the fraud.

'Except my appearance, I suppose,' Philip managed to say, with the bitterness of despair in his voice.

'Yes,' Dr Armstrong agreed, intervening. 'I am sure Dr Shore found no difference in you when Mrs Bennet turned up again. She telephoned to him, remember, to announce her return and to ask him to meet her at Garwood. She must have been entirely satisfied with your likeness to – to–'

'The thing in the tin box that I thought was a cat,' Philip said, and added, 'if I hadn't insisted on digging it up again the other day–'

'If you had declared the find the first time you dug it up, the fraud might have been laid bare then, and your upbringing would have been very different,' McNee told him in his dry, elderly voice.

'Better if I'd never dug it up at all!'

'Perhaps, though the truth has many ways of struggling to the light, however dark it lies,' the lawyer pronounced.

'If it helps to find Mrs Bennet's murderer it will really be a blessing,' Dr Armstrong put in quickly. 'Quite apart from discovering your real parentage, which may go with it. Holmes will tell you so himself and that he is very grateful for the exposure.'

Philip's overwhelming distress turned to fury. Speechless, he banged a fist on the table beside him, jarred his freshly healed forearm, yelled his protest at the sharp pain that shot from fist to shoulder and jumping to his feet, rushed out of the room.

Miss Tupper spoke for the first time since the two professionals began to deliver their news.

'He'll be all right,' she said. 'He's naturally very sensitive. But quite stable. You know that, don't you, Dr Armstrong? It's appalling for him, of course, no name, no property, no position, except junior master at a smallish prep school. To face all that, after what he thought he had. No parents, no relations, simply nothing at all, but what he has taken for granted for the twenty-two years of almost his whole life.'

Detective Superintendent Holmes, when he called again at Garwood that evening, was more positive in his views and more hopeful. Without disclosing how he knew it, he explained to Philip that evidence had come to light showing that Mrs Bennet, as the actress Maisie Atkins, had taken the packet from Weymouth to St Malo, but had not returned that way, though she had taken back her car, parked near the port, six days later, arriving at Garwood the same day. Where had she been in France? Presumably

189

not at any holiday resort in the north, if she had been looking for work of a theatrical kind. More likely Paris or even the Riviera. They were in touch with Interpol. Difficult so long after. But worth a try.

Philip listened, stony-faced. It was not his mother who had been murdered. The woman he had always loved for her pretty face, caring for him, guiding him; whom he had never really understood, seldom admired for her intellect or opinions; this woman had most grossly betrayed him. She was a fraud, a criminal. She had used him for her own criminal purposes. So why should he continue to do the work of the police for them?

'You never went abroad together, did you?' Holmes asked.

'Never. Scotland, Wales, south coast places, Channel Islands twice, Southampton to Peter Port.'

'So she never needed a passport? Did she have one?'

'I don't know. I never saw one. I've got one, of course. I've been to France with college friends, twice, and to Austria, Vienna. Oh, and to ski in Switzerland, twice.'

'May I see your passport?'

'Sure.'

Everything was in order. Holmes did not stay long. He was as surprised as most people at the long-standing success of the old welsher. Suppose the baby *had* died on her, which sounded the most likely explanation of the death, her plan of action, immediate, without hesitation, complete in all the detail, had been masterly. She had brought it off. It was ironical that it had been blown by the person least likely to do so deliberately.

Who must now be cursing himself for his action, poor lad. So, of all those she had injured or frustrated by her fraud which one had finally caught up with her and exacted the ultimate price? From here or from abroad? From Canada or the Continent?

Was he really any nearer to the answer?

13

After one more interview with Detective Superintendent Holmes Miss Tupper left Broxbourne and drove back to her own home in an anxious and thoughtful mood. The death of her old friend, old in time rather than age, had been a shock: the discovery of that friend's considerable fraud and cruel deceit gave an added shock and grief, to which the need for continued secrecy was no less painful for being absolutely necessary.

For, as Holmes pointed out, the whole affair had grown from a baffling, but limited and local domestic incident, with fatal violence, or perhaps petty blackmail disappointed, again with violence, or perhaps a local grievance with misplaced, brutal revenge, to a large-scale conspiracy to defraud, successful for over twenty years. But, with a typical falling-out of thieves, beginning now to crumble. How often gang murder did split open these partnerships in crime, Holmes concluded, shaking his head.

Miss Tupper was not deceived. Mr Holmes was inwardly rejoicing, she saw clearly. He now thought Florence had been guided all along by others much better qualified in crime than herself. Given the original child had died on her, as seemed very probable, some person or persons had pointed out that with the husband dead too she would be penniless without the heir to Garwood. So this partner or gang had found her an heir. It was up to him, with the French police, if necessary, to find this partner or group.

Holmes listened to Miss Tupper's conclusions. He assured her that there was very much more hope now of finding a satisfactory answer to all the outstanding questions. He would keep her informed.

So Miss Tupper drove away home to Kent, not agreeing with Holmes, because she felt she knew Florence better than he did, and that the failed actress had qualities, quite outside acting talent, that could explain how she had managed entirely without other assistance.

One thing she did agree with. Florence must have fled away abroad when the baby died, after burying it with swift, but loving care. She must have got the news of Percy's death while abroad, probably looking for work. And that had turned her mind to claiming Garwood, provided she had a baby boy on whose behalf to claim the estate.

Looking for work then, first. Where?

Before she reached her cottage, Miss Tupper had decided upon this. *Italy.* Why had she not thought of it before? Of course.

At least one tour, in which she herself had taken part. No, *two*. The second one without herself in the party. Naples. Yes, Naples: after Genoa, the year before.

Pip had said that Florence had never gone anywhere abroad, or rather away from England, where she needed a passport. She must have had a passport when she was Maisie Atkins. And one for her honeymoon, surely? Or was she on Percy's passport for that?

Miss Tupper made up her mind while she was still on the road. She would go to Naples herself. She would not tell the police of her intention, in case they either forbade her or got there first. Besides, if they ran down Eleanora, yes, that was the splendid theatrical landlady's name, her first name, she wouldn't tell them anything. Eleanora had been a young girl in Mussolini's Italy. She must hate and fear the police even now, as she did then. The only way to get Eleanora's confidence was to visit her as an old friend, an old, retired actress.

So very quietly, telling her local friends merely that she felt she needed a rest, a holiday from the continuing shock and problems of poor Florence's unsolved murder and the subsequent terrible fire at the dead woman's house, she stopped her milk and her newspapers for a week, drove herself to Gatwick, parked her car there for the week and flew direct to Naples. Feeling quite proud of herself she ordered a taxi to take her to the house whose address she had found among her old diaries.

The house was still there, just where she remembered it, in a narrow street where the washing lines of the upper apartments were strung between the houses, like decorations in England at some public festival or national rejoicing.

Eleanora was there, too, and remembered her. But it was many years since Aunt Amy had used the Italian language and though she had been fluent enough in her theatre days to get bit parts in Italian, she found her former landlady hard to understand now and herself speechless, except in English.

However, one or two English-speaking Italians came to their assistance.

'So you are the lady for the older parts, the dignified, the betrayed, maybe, the beat-up?'

'Quite often the comic, making a fool of myself, to get a laugh from the gallery.'

'And Signorita Atkins, so beautiful, like a girl from Napoli herself, black hair and so dark eyes. So unhappy, no money, no job. And nothing for her here nothing at all.'

'You do remember her then, when she came looking for work? It was over twenty years ago. You are sure you remember?'

'I have been thinking of her a good many

196

days. It was mentioned in English television news, and an old photo. She had married and had one son. The husband was dead – an accident many years ago. The murderer is not yet found?'

'Not yet.' Miss Tupper paused. Perhaps it was enough to have established that Maisie had indeed come to Naples at the beginning of her flight. But she wanted to know more. She wanted to know what Maisie had been doing in Naples. Had she stayed there all five days? How had she spent the time? Dear old Eleanora might know a bit more.

'Out all day,' the old woman said, enjoying this plunge into the past. It was like old times, chatting with this English actress from so many years ago. 'Maisie was in poor shape when she come to my door. She had two suitcases, good ones, newish, and good clothes on her back. But she looked–' the interpreter searched for a strong word, 'she looked in despair. She said she was that, too.'

'Desperate, you mean? For money?'

'Not exactly. But none coming in, you understand? She paid me for a full week's board and lodging straight off, in Italian money.'

'Straight off? Do you mean she had Italian lira in her purse when she arrived?'

Eleanora stared.

'But yes. She paid the taxi. She also gave

me lira. Does it matter?'

'Not a bit,' Miss Tupper said hurriedly. Nor did it, she thought. The airport could exchange her travellers' cheque. She could have got any particular currency before her sudden flight. But Holmes had told her Maisie had cashed a cheque from Percy, drawing it all in travellers' cheques, though ostensibly only going to Bournemouth.

'Miss Atkins was well dressed, too,' Eleanora repeated. 'I wondered at that. She was certainly desperate for a job, those first two days. Going to the agents, asking round at the theatres. She'd have taken anything, in any line, to get a living wage.'

'But she didn't find anything?'

'Not in Naples, no. But a job, oh dear me, yes. The excitement, that third day! In Rome, she said. That was when she found the job and went off in a taxi to the station with her two suitcases early the next morning.'

'Did you see her off at the station?'

'Not me. No time for idling around in the early morning, waving goodbye to you theatre people.' The stout woman laughed. 'She got off all right. Her driver put her down at the station and saw her start to go in, with the usual swarm of porters round her.'

'Very different in England now,' Miss Tupper could not help saying. 'You can't get a porter, even at London stations; helping anyone is beneath their exalted ideas of their status, as they call it.'

On this sour note the conversation came to an end. But Miss Tupper had not concluded her researches. She engaged a room at Eleanora's for two nights and after settling in and having a late lunch of pasta, a peach and coffee, made a preliminary tour of the theatrical agents and the theatres. At none of these could she find any record of Maisie's enquiries. They simply told her that their records did not go back so far. Oh, yes, they knew what productions had been put on at that time, which had succeeded, and which had flopped. They did know what English bookings they had made, with a few notes of names they might engage again. But enquiries for work? Really! And not successful, either! How could one expect–?

How indeed! She did not expect, but she would have liked to know. Only one agency had the courtesy to look up the day books, but with no real light to give.

'Yes, Signora. The old books are still on our shelves, under all the old headings. Travel, the most important here, local, national and international. Entertainment. Opera. Theatre and of course, circus, the original firm, the name of the founder and still in the third generation, still at work–'

'Theatre,' said Aunt Amy, interrupting the

girl, who had begun to turn the pages of the firm's history with real interest. 'Theatre. That's where you will find Miss Atkins. In the late autumn of 1953. No mention of that name? Nothing to do with Maisie Atkins?'

'Nothing, Signora.'

The girl closed the books, putting them back in their correct order. Miss Tupper congratulated her upon the careful and accurate method used in these records.

'As a rule,' the girl said, as they turned away, 'but it seemed to have failed just where we needed it.'

An older colleague made no excuse, but explained the apparent lapse.

'There was a serious family calamity at about that time,' she said. 'A very serious family loss. I had only just joined the business in the travel office and showroom. I remember the senior partners were away for nearly a month. Probably that is why your friend didn't have the attention she would normally expect.'

Then where, Aunt Amy asked herself, did Maisie get the tip-off for Rome? She continued her search, but found nothing. So, with promises to come back to Naples upon a happier errand in the future, Miss Tupper took the train north to continue her search in the Italian capital.

But with no better result. No agent of any kind had dealt with a good-looking English actress in her early thirties. Records of all operas and plays performed that autumn season in Rome were easy to find: there was nothing that remotely could have included Maisie. Simply nothing at all, there or on tour in any part of Italy. Miss Tupper knew that her resources did not cover any further research. So she flew back to England to report to Detective Superintendent Holmes.

He was less than enthusiastic.

'If I had known of your intention,' he said stiffly, 'I could have helped, through the Italian police.'

'Which is precisely why I didn't let you know,' she snapped back. 'Our dear old Eleanora. She must be nearly a hundred. She wasn't young when Maisie and I first knew her. She would have a dozen fits if their intelligence lot went for her. But she knew me at once and she told me all about Maisie's four days with her up to the time she left for Rome. She was alone all that time.'

'No baby?'

'No. Maisie was alone, told Eleanora nothing, not even that she was married, so not her married name. Simply that she needed a job.'

After a pause Holmes said, 'So what we really need to know is where Mrs Bennet found the news of Mr Bennet's death, Naples or Rome. In an English newspaper or an Italian one?'

'Probably English. Maisie's Italian was rusty, like mine, I expect. Why is it important where she found it?'

'Because we need to know where to look for a missing baby, in Rome or in Naples.'

'Of course.'

Miss Tupper was ashamed of herself. She might have understood this before, while she was in Italy. She said as much.

'I think we, with Interpol, have wider facilities than you have, Miss Tupper.' Holmes was inclined to be indulgent. 'Family matters, domestic events, of an unnatural kind–'

All right, Miss Tupper said to herself, if you must be so smug, you can get on with it. But when he had gone, she sat down at her desk in the cottage and wrote, in rather poor Italian, to Eleanora to explain her latest conclusion, which was that Maisie Atkins's death might possibly be connected with a family disaster in Naples at, or just after, or just before, the actress's visit. Could Eleanora tell her of any such? Particularly if it concerned the big firm of Luccini, those agents Maisie had visited to ask for help.

Miss Tupper also wrote to Mrs Harper to ask if the work of restoration was going on well. In connection with the worst affected part of the house, she wrote, Mrs Bennet's so-called office, she wondered if much there had been destroyed entirely. Also whether Pip had been down to Garwood again, to sort out his mother's papers and so on. Those, of course, that had not been destroyed, but only partly burned.

Mrs Harper replied to that letter by return of post. She was very worried, she wrote. Mr Pip had not been home, though there were many things that needed his word to start being done. Instead Mr McNee, the solicitor, had been, with a written order from Mr Pip, to take away any papers belonging to Mrs Bennet. He had gone through the office, though there was nothing much there worth saving. The wall safe had been well roasted, nothing but ash in it when the men got it open. News in the village that Reg Somerton had been at sea on the night of the fire, doing a job of work for a change. She did hope, she concluded, as she began, that Mr Pip would come home to stay when his school term ended.

What Mrs Harper did not put in her letter to Miss Tupper related to her further conduct on the day of Mr McNee's visit. She had resented the solicitor's manner; it seemed strangely inconsiderate to Mr Pip, seeing the solicitor was the family's man, or so she had always understood.

So it seemed to Mrs Harper, when the lawyer had gone away, that it was her personal concern to place in safety, for the young master's own and sole disposal, those special treasures and mementoes as she always thought of them, that Mrs Bennet had lodged with herself in the week following Mr Pip's coming of age, the proper week at twenty-one, not the legal one at eighteen. This box, not large, was fastened round with a strap, but not locked in any way.

After Mr McNee had gone, Mrs Harper went to her own rooms, which had been undamaged, and took from the back of one cupboard that collection of treasures she had so far withheld from the police as being none of their concern. She had never thought of opening it: indeed she had forgotten its existence in the turmoil of the murder and the fire, with the total upsetting of that tranquil life into which she had built her own from middle-age.

But Mr McNee's manner, so grave, so urgent, so apparently independent of Mr Pip's interest, had frightened her. And the young master himself: even before the fire, that nasty find in the shrubbery still not explained–

She turned to her beloved mistress's box of mementoes, as she had always called it, with acute nostalgia, not without a certain dread. She undid the strap, she opened the box. Among a hotchpotch of old letters, old theatre programmes, old photographs, she found a smallish, blue, gold-patterned booklet. She recognised it as a passport and deciding that such things were certainly not private, being designed for use and display all over the world, she opened it and turned the pages.

The last entry engaged her attention. Mrs Bennet had travelled from Naples to Heathrow on a date she would always remember, that of her own arrival at Garwood. No, three days *after* her own arrival in 1953, in time to see the master, only a few hours before his tragic accident and death.

So they had come from Italy? That was why the little love, at her first sight of him, had looked so well, so brown and blooming. They had taken a short holiday in the south, had they? In the sun. Naturally enough, to get away from the late English autumn, all rain and frost and fog.

Well, what now? Mrs Harper knew there had been a mystery over this holiday. Why? It was natural enough. Only Mr Bennet seemed so upset, because he had been away in London when she set out, and he had thought she was going to Bournemouth and she hadn't told him of her change of plan. Mrs Bennet herself never explained this to anyone, it seems. Why need she?

All the same, Mr Holmes kept asking about those missing days. She herself had thought of them. It was not her place to expect confidences from her employer, though they had always been friends. The village had nearly forgotten the whole affair, except of course Mrs Somerton.

Now she had this answer. The passport. In the name of Florence Bennet and the baby. Philip Montague Bennet, on his mother's document. Mrs Harper went to the telephone to bring this news to those she considered had the right to have it.

The duty constable at the Incident Centre in Broxbourne, hearing a fresh note of urgency in the housekeeper's voice, promised to convey her request to the detective superintendent at once, and did so before returning to his gambling calculations.

Detective Superintendent Holmes was at Garwood House three hours later.

14

Matters in the Bennet murder case began to move more briskly. Holmes felt he had, at last, a real lead towards an adequate motive for the crime.

The two pieces of solid evidence had come to him almost simultaneously. Miss Tupper had given him, as a fact that could be proved, the arrival of Mrs Bennet, as the actress Maisie Atkins, at the house of a theatrical landlady in Naples. Mrs Harper had given him a long-concealed passport, the last entry in which proved that Mrs Bennet, as the wife of Percy Bennet, together with her four-month-old baby, had flown out from Naples to Heathrow, on the morning of the day before she turned up again at Pullen's garage near Weymouth. In the afternoon of that day, she had arrived at Garwood. She had been Maisie Atkins, childless and seemingly unmarried, when she left Weymouth Harbour on her outward voyage. She had been a newly widowed woman with a child when she arrived in England. She had claimed her car the next morning in the same guise she had adopted when parking it.

A big step gained. Philip must, almost certainly, have been an Italian baby, or rather a baby adopted or stolen or even *bought,* in Naples.

That formerly-thought impossible motive, revenge, flashed up again in the detective's mind. A mother, perhaps as distraught as Mrs Bennet's letter to Miss Tupper had been, longing to be rid of a child who was too much for her, in work and responsibility? A family appalled at this callous disposal. A life-long hunt for the despoiler. A patient hunt. Italians in England. Modern methods of communication?

Holmes's mind burst into a shower of speculation like a Guy Fawkes firework. He assembled his facts and while Detective Sergeant Tom Miles began a tour of Weymouth hotels, with the assistance of the local uniformed police, others continued to examine Joe Pullen's police records and the books of his firm and the records of his bank accounts, one for the firm and one private.

He himself renewed his appeal to Interpol. He had much more to ask them, the whole story of where Mrs Bennet could have found her substitute child in Naples. Not openly. In fact, very secretly, for the Italian landlady had not been told. This woman had been led to believe that Miss Atkins, as she still called herself, had not been mixed up in any conspiracy. She had gone, childless, by taxi, to the station for Rome.

Instead of taking the train she had boarded a plane at Naples, shortly afterwards, that same morning, for London.

Interpol promised to look into this twenty-two-year-old theft or criminal bargain, relating to an Italian subject, a four-month-old male. Certainly, the thief was worthy of pursuit and exposure and punishment. The woman was dead? Well, she deserved it. Revenge? Justified. All the same – Interpol would co-operate. But it was a very long time ago, was it not?

Meanwhile Mr McNee, ignorant of these developments, was still intent upon clearing up the complicated matter of the disposal of the Garwood estate, for his duties as executor of Percy Bennet's will had come back upon him in full force, with young Philip's necessary, but not yet legalised, or openly declared, disinheritance.

Bruce McNee was a very worried man. He had always acted and worked in favour of order; calm, unhurried order, just conclusions, fair dealing. For years he had held off the eager Thorntons, with their hankering for at least a share in the Garwood properties. Percy's sister had a good deal of his greed, perhaps even more, for where he had preserved his wealth by saving it up, she had been frankly acquisitive. It was she who watched her brother very carefully, being a few years older than he was. Until she married, in her middle thirties, well before he did, and went to Canada with her husband, she had kept in touch with the staff at Garwood. She knew all about Mrs Somerton's child. She had been terrified Percy might marry the woman. That hurdle surmounted, though only in abeyance, since the housekeeper was back in office in less than a year, with young Reg palmed off to his grandparents in the village.

But Mrs Thornton felt secure enough to stay in Canada until the unexpected happened. Percy married at last! Worst blow of all his bride was a young, or youngish woman, and within a year produced that threatened heir, to ruin her expectations for ever.

This was now Mr McNee went over the history of the Thorntons in his mind as he set about the most distasteful task of announcing his dreadful news. Dreadful, in its huge, alarming dishonesty, its terrifying simplicity; the impossibility of any real redress for those injured, of whom the prime victim was poor Philip, that wretched young man, whose whole life till now had been proved a lie, an imposture.

Philip had gone back to his school, determined to give notice and leave at the end of term. If possible the Press and media could be kept at bay a bit longer. Philip wanted this; that non-relative and formidable lady, Aunt Amy, wanted it; the police wanted it urgently, as they followed up a host of new clues to Mrs Bennet's well-hidden past. But would the Thorntons play ball? McNee thought he might rely on Thornton himself, who had always considered Garwood a bit of a joke. But the son called 'Tig'? A nasty piece of work, Mr McNee considered him; very hairy, scruffy, foul-mouthed. No feeling for the family. Well, could you blame him? He was Thornton, not Bennet, and had seldom been in England for more than a few days at a time, when 'doing Europe'.

But Mrs Thornton? That was another story. She would be out for blood to the last drop. To think that she had been done out of Garwood, the whole estate, for over twenty years and had been made to accept its ultimate complete loss! Mr McNee shuddered to think of the probable extent of her malice and to wonder how those savings of Mrs Bennet's could be preserved for the now penniless young Philip.

Fortunately the older Thornton was still in London after leaving Dorset before the latest discoveries. His wife had gone back to Canada. Tig was somewhere this side of the Atlantic, on a limited allowance, his father said, and would turn up in due course.

Mr McNee managed to compose an

entirely uninformative letter, but one which stressed the importance of an early interview respecting the Garwood estate.

Mr Thornton replied by telephone, naming a time and date and place. He spoke to Mr McNee's office number and to the solicitor's clerk, who made the appointment in his principal's absence. But, as Mr Thornton explained, he was leaving London the next day after that date to join his son in Paris, so the interview would be delayed, if not convenient, for perhaps two weeks.

Mr McNee looked at the dates, wondering what Tig had been doing in Paris; wondering too, if the interview would ever take place before the horribly melodramatic story would break from some other source than his, or the murderer be discovered, with a similar result. He felt dispirited.

Then there was the mystery of the fire. Reg Somerton was the obvious name for its originator. That young scamp's history of crime had built up from his school days. He had been known to start several fires, unsuccessful as major acts of arson, but damaging enough in the part loss of a house, with much-loved if not very valuable contents, or a garage complete with car, or part of a farmyard with animals trapped in the blaze.

But Garwood's fire could not have been

Reg's work, for though his whereabouts were undiscovered directly after the blaze, the search for him was undertaken with increasing seriousness. He then disappointed the police of several counties by turning up in Poole Harbour aboard a small cargo boat with coal from the east coast.

Then why had no one in Broxbourne seemed to know where Reg had been? Why had his mother been so particularly reticent on this occasion? Certainly she had usually pretended not to know where he was when they wanted him, but this time she could only help him. Detective Superintendent Holmes went to see her.

'Reg home now, Mrs Somerton?' he asked her. 'Enjoyed his trip on the briny?'

The old woman stared at him, her eyes bright with malice, her old mouth twisting sourly.

'You've always got it in for him, Mr Holmes, haven't you? Yes, I knew he was on a ship, going steady, and not a day too soon. Out of your clutches for once, you and your lot. How he chooses to work is his business, when it's honest, as this was.'

Her voice went up and down in a sing-song fashion, very hard to take, Holmes thought. But he let her run on until she fell to mumbling abuse of her neighbours as well as of the police force, her own hard lot and the weather.

Then he said, 'It was because we want to know who gave the warning to the Fire Brigade first-off, before Mr Bennet realised the house was burning and went to the phone himself. We thought maybe Reg had put through that first call; he might just have seen the blaze, not having made it, not concerned with making it, but wanting to stop it. But he couldn't have been there, could he, because he was actually on that coal boat at the time, and we know that from his ship's captain as well as himself.'

'Then why do you go on so?' asked Mrs Somerton, very reasonably. 'Why come to me?'

'Who else could have been out in the night near Garwood and watched an arsonist, or helped an arsonist at work, until the fire had taken hold, and then realised their duty and made a call. It came from Broxbourne, one of the public boxes, we do know that.'

Mrs Somerton was silent, perhaps considering all of her friends and enemies.

'Well,' Holmes said at last, 'can you help me, Mrs Somerton?'

But she did not answer, only sat and stared, with malice and hatred and a kind of slow triumph in her small old eyes.

Philip was spared the embarrassment of resigning his post at short notice for no very adequate reason by the Headmaster himself, and that only two days after he went back to work.

The Head had been worried that his action would look callous if he broke his contract with the boy just after his misfortune, his double calamity of the loss of a large part of his house and his personal injuries. But since neither of these ills had been crippling and Philip Bennet, though unnaturally subdued, did not seem to have suffered very severely, he thought he had better go ahead to avoid blame, while minds were on other matters of more general importance.

Philip took the delicately-phrased dismissal with calm acceptance. In fact he welcomed it. He need only listen to the Head's excuses and explanations, his own lack of academic teaching ability, his rather dangerous excellence in the gym, his domestic duties, that would increase, that had flared (unfortunate word) in the immediate past. Philip would know what he meant.

Philip, keeping unexpected laughter under control, said he fully understood. In fact he did not think he would have stayed for more than a term in any case.

The Head, grateful for the ease of this agreement, produced a glass of sherry to mark his gratitude. He suggested that the rest of the staff be told that Philip would not return in the autumn and that in this way the news would leak gently over the whole school in the usual way. His end-of-the-school-year letter to the parents would inform them officially, and the boys would learn it as more than a rumour, in the school mag., even before the official school breaking-up assembly.

Philip sipped his sherry, wondering if the larger, devastating disclosure about his junior assistant master would fall upon the Head before that breaking-up meeting for the summer holidays. He hoped not until the poor old pompous, well-meaning, shrewd, boy-knowing, parent-fearing so-and-so had escaped to the Brittany coast, where he usually spent the long summer holidays.

Where would he be spending them himself? Somewhere remote, he decided. And alone. It was impossible now to attempt to continue any sort of relationship with Lotta. No good feeling she was more than half his life: there could, there must not, be any joy there. He had decided before the final blow, after her repentant appearance at the hospital, that she was definitely his girl and he would marry her. Perhaps not until she had taken her finals. Now more than ever until she had taken them and could earn, he told himself cynically. No, there was no question of marriage now or in the future. Damn it, she was only just twenty.

He decided to allow their twice-weekly

letters or phone calls to lapse. He supposed he had better invent a new surname and take himself abroad. Was he European? In his present savage mood he tried to assess his physical make-up. Average height, strong build, dark wavy hair, very dark eyes, brownish, not sallow, complexion. So possibly Mediterranean, rather than Northern European. What about Middle Eastern? Or even North Asian?

He occupied his spare time for the rest of the term with tennis, squash, swimming and athletics. He was a very unhappy young man, in no way reconciled to his fate.

15

Carlotta Moorehead, at home, was not at all inclined to accept another era of silence. The first had been her own fault: she had acknowledged that and thought it had been washed out. Not a bit of it. Phil had not phoned; he had not written. He was always 'not available' at his school. Mrs Harper was sorry, Mr Pip was out or Mr Pip was away from home. Even Miss Tupper, as a last resort, proved to be abroad, on a much-needed summer holiday, her transferred number reported.

In the end, about two weeks after the end of the school term, Carlotta could bear the maddening silence no longer. O.K., if Phil wanted it off, so be it, but let's be civilised over it. If he had decided she was boring him or he'd come up with some super-smashing new dish, she'd take that and get over it. But she'd got to know, hadn't she?

All this Carlotta poured out to her mother one evening, when she had refused a promising party in the immediate neighbourhood because Philip might ring up. He had not done so.

Mrs Moorehead had a clear idea of the

cause of her daughter's bad temper, restless idleness and sulky expression. So at ten o'clock, Mr Moorehead being at a late meeting of the committee of his billiards club, she left her unhappy child staring into the twilit garden, made two cups of cocoa, put a generous helping of rum in each and took them back to the sitting room.

It was a cool evening, after much-needed summer rain.

'*Hot* drink?' Carlotta said in a disgusted voice.

'Drink it up,' her mother ordered. 'Early bed is what you need. Too much gadding about lately.'

'*Gadding!*'

Carlotta was defeated. The rum thawed the ice in her heart. She gulped it down and burst into tears of mingled rage, hurt pride and fear. Afterwards she explained this.

'I thought I knew what was worrying him,' she sobbed. 'First the murder then the fire. But it all seems to have just died down and he's always not available, as they call it.'

Mrs Moorehead found it difficult to take her young daughter's latest romance very seriously. It was by no means the first; she was still only just twenty. She never lacked for friends, particularly, in these days, boyfriends. There would surely be many more. But the disappointments, the sharp griefs, of the young, could be heart-rending while they lasted. Besides, Carlotta shared her own Italian blood; her feelings were of a Mediterranean shape and size. So she held her daughter in comforting arms and suggested they might drive about Dorset, with dad as well, next weekend and perhaps pay a visit to Garwood in the course of their tour.

Carlotta was suspicious; was her mother intent on vetting Phil's estate, before confirming her truer sympathy? Well, never mind if she was. Parents had these mercenary, cynically interested ideas. Nice Mrs Harper might help, at least.

Mr Moorehead fell in with the idea, but without great enthusiasm. However he agreed to go to the coast of Dorset on Friday, and on Saturday offered the car to Carlotta to enable her to visit her friend, leaving him and her mother at Lulworth Cove.

Garwood House showed no outward signs of its recent ordeal by fire. Nor did Mrs Harper, who opened the front door herself.

'Oh, Miss Moorehead,' she said. 'I did hope you'd call. If I'd had your address, I'd have written.'

Her distress was obvious; Carlotta felt a sudden chill.

'Isn't he here?' she asked. 'I felt sure he must be. He isn't ill?'

'Not ill. No, the burns hardly show now. Not ill, but not himself. Oh, Miss Lotta, I've been so worried!'

'Can't I see him?' Carlotta was becoming frantic.

'He's down by the tennis court, most likely,' Mrs Harper said. 'But he won't see visitors. I've to say the house is not fit for visitors after the fire.'

'He's bloody well going to see *me!*' the girl burst out and was away, running across the grass, her hair flying, her bag swinging. Past the shady trees, past the fatal shrubbery, round the corner to the lower garden and the tennis court. Running, jumping down the bordering bank, she dodged the balls Philip was driving across the net. And when he saw her, driving directly at her in exasperated fury.

She leaped a low spin, dodged another, shouted, 'Stop it, you nit! You damn fool! You'll kill me!'

She reached him, flung away her bag and as he dropped his racquet, rushed into his arms and lay against him, panting.

She could not have forced his confidence more effectively, Philip decided later, and told her so. This was after a very complete physical reconciliation, when they lay exhausted, but happy, in the shade beside the tennis court.

Carlotta could find no words for her astonishment, but she did not in any way share Philip's despair.

'I think it's rather exciting,' she said. She had a tendency to giggle.

He said sourly, 'Super, as we used to say at school. My real mother must have been a pretty lousy mum, foisting me off. Illigit., I suppose. Careless bint, prostitute, maybe?'

'Why any of that?' Carlotta was indignant. 'Probably a respectable couple with a late mistake they couldn't face rearing. Or why not from an adoption home, parents both killed in an accident?'

'Then why not acknowledge that? No, of course, this place and the money.'

Philip's features contracted again in renewed grief, disgust and weary despair. He rolled over, hiding his face in his arms, inconsolable.

After a while Carlotta said, in what she hoped was a normal voice, 'Look, my parents are at Lulworth for the day. I've got to go back and pick them up. Can we go in and get Harpie to make us a cup of tea and then you come over to Lulworth to meet mum and dad.'

He looked at her with sulky suspicion.

'Bountiful little lady bringing nameless waif into happy home?'

She smacked his face as hard as she could, which led naturally to further amorous wrestling, after which they did as she proposed.

But not until, after tea, Carlotta suggested they might go through the nursery cupboards to see if they could find any of Philip's early toys.

In this they were partly successful, because there was one fragment that Carlotta recognised.

'It's part of a toy,' she said. 'I had one from Italy, something like it. A wheelbarrow? My mother might know what it is. We'll ask her if you like.'

They told Mrs Harper of their find, asking her if any more of his early toys had survived the fire.

'Not the nursery things, only what you've been through, Mr Pip. But I have a box of oddments Mrs Bennet gave me to keep safe for her, years ago, that was. Mementoes and such. I think you ought to have it.'

'Yes. I think I ought.'

Philip spoke strangely. Mrs Harper wondered what she had done wrong. She became defensive. Police or no police she wasn't going to put herself in the wrong with her young master.

'You see, I went through it only the other day, tidying my own cupboards after my things went back into my rooms. I took the liberty of asking Mr Holmes to look at the old passport that was with them—'

'You *what?*'

'Oh, Mr Pip, if I've done wrong you must make allowance. There's nothing private about a passport that I can see and nothing that shouldn't be known about this one. And it did just give the date of the last time it was used, which was when your mother brought you home after your father was killed.'

'Where *from?*' Carlotta asked, unsteadily, for Philip had gone very white and seemed unable to speak.

'Napoli – that's Naples – in Italy, isn't it, Miss Lotta?'

Mrs Harper spoke with dignity. As neither of the young people seemed capable of speech, but both looked shocked and strained, she added, 'I do hope you don't think I did wrong, Mr Pip. Mr Holmes was pleased to have it. He kept it. He said it belonged to the government.'

'Correct,' said Philip, pulling himself together. He looked at the housekeeper's worried face and felt sudden contrition for the way he was behaving. So he put his arms round her and kissed her tenderly.

'Dear Harpie,' he said, 'of course you did right. As always, you always help, don't you?'

The Mooreheads were not at all surprised to see their daughter arriving with a young man who fitted her usual, rather perfunctory description of him. Philip Bennet. Naturally she introduced him as Phil, without a surname.

But when Mr Moorehead tactfully suggested a swim or else a walk on the cliffs while his daughter brought matters up to date with her mother, Philip chose the latter, saying he had not taken nearly enough exercise since the end of term.

With the men out of the way Carlotta explained Phil's terrible position. Mrs Moorehead was very genuinely shocked and her first thoughts were all for him.

'Poor unlucky boy!' she exclaimed. 'What a perfectly frightful thing! Coming like this, just after his mother was killed!'

'Only she wasn't his mother,' Carlotta corrected angrily. 'Only some rotten bitch, grabbing a fortune by snatching him or forcing him or *buying* him from weak-kneed real parents or a money-grabbing adoption agency.'

'And she did this, apparently, in Naples,' Mrs Moorehead said, thoughtfully. 'At least you say her passport shows she flew from there with the baby straight to Heathrow.'

They stared at one another.

'You always seem to forget that I am Italian,' Mrs Moorehead said gently. 'And what's more to the point, we're going touring round the Lakes a week from now. All of us, I think.'

'You mean–'

'Carlotta, my darling, are you serious about this young man? Is he serious about you?'

'How do I know? Well, yes, more than anyone else, so far. But sorry for him over Mrs Bennet – I never actually met her – and over the fire and of course more than ever over this.'

'For his own sake or because he loses everything he seemed to own?'

'*Mother!* Don't be horrible!'

'It makes a difference if the boy-friend can supply all the food and the transport and the parties, without getting in the red. I'm not too old to remember these things, though at home in Italy–'

'Not *again!* I do remember about your childhood.'

As her mother looked hurt, Carlotta mumbled, 'I'm sorry. I don't know what I'm saying today. Oh, hell, here they are, back! What next?'

'You tell him you've told me, while I tell daddy. Then we go up to the hotel for dinner in the garden and discuss how we can help him to find his lost Italian family.'

If Philip resented this open, this widened view of his position, he made no protest, no effort to escape back to Garwood and total secrecy. Instead he felt a release from the unbearable tension and with it a much calmer, less self-pitying estimate of the chances of real discovery, both of the reason for the murder and the identity of his own parents.

They had settled for their intimate conversation, with coffee and brandy, in a more secluded part of the hotel garden than the open space, with small tables and umbrellas, where they had eaten their dinner. Here their talk could not be overheard and they would see any other visitors approaching.

It was Mr Moorehead, anticipating his wife's suggestion, who proposed carrying research to Naples itself.

'We usually like to wander round the Lakes because my wife comes from the north and those southern towns, even on the sea, are much too hot in August. But local newspapers would be the thing. Find out if there was a local incident twenty years ago, involving an orphaned child.'

'Hospitals, too, same sort of thing, surely?' said Carlotta.

'The police are on to Interpol,' Philip told them. 'They will cover all that, won't they?'

'Perhaps,' Mr Moorehead agreed. 'If you'd like to join us, Philip?'

'You're very kind.' Philip was too much moved by the offer to be able to say more. But after a minute or two he explained. 'I'd love to, but I don't speak Italian. I suppose I ought to learn – it seems so extraordinary – if I'm really Italian–'

'We'll teach you,' Carlotta broke in.

'Let him finish,' ordered her father.

228

'Actually I've been deciding I'd better get a job at a sports centre or something. I'm reasonably, well, moderately well qualified in gym, only they don't have the apparatus at prep schools.'

'I should hope not,' Mr Moorehead said, and laughed.

'So I've booked myself at an advanced school of gym – acrobatics, really. The Olympics, you know. Those Iron Curtain kids a few years back. Marvellous. We've got plenty of material here, if we can only get hold of it early enough, I mean young enough. I'm a bit old for it now, but I've been trying out stunts for years. Only my mother wasn't all that keen–'

Mr Moorehead nodded. He approved of the boy's intention and of his energy in setting out so sensibly to realise it. He did not press him to join them, but he determined to make their search a success if that was in any way possible.

It was then that Carlota remembered the old toy. She jumped up suddenly and ran away to the car park, coming back at once with the small battered remnant in her hand.

'We found it in the old nursery,' she explained. 'Phil doesn't remember it, but we think it must have come from Italy, because he had it with him when he arrived at Garwood.'

Mrs Moorehead looked at it and shook

her head. She passed it on to her husband.

'Bit of a little model farm cart, wood, painted, I think,' he decided, turning it over, carefully. 'But not Italian, I think. German, more likely.'

'Austrian, could it be?' Mrs Moorehead looked disappointed. 'Not from Naples, you think?'

Philip put out a hand for it.

'Never mind,' he said. 'I'll take it in to Holmes. Give him another think about the Naples story. Who's to say my parents weren't German tourists, or refugee Jews?'

'Who's to say it didn't come from a toy stall at Heathrow?' said Carlotta.

16

Disregarding the older Mooreheads' feelings about the Naples climate in summer, the family spent their first week abroad by travelling in their own car to that southern centre of arrival for tourists. Instead of taking off at once for the island of Capri or in local tours to Vesuvius, both the mountain crater and the wonderfully preserved towns at its foot, or along the sensational mountain roads of the coast line to Amalfi, Mr Moorehead organised fishing trips for himself and his son while his womenfolk searched the newspaper agents and offices for stored copies of ancient date.

Because Mrs Moorehead was clearly of Italian birth and spoke the language with a slightly alien, but cultivated, north Italian accent, she found her quest sympathetically understood. Italy had been in a confused state for years after the Second World War. In 1953 there were still frequent cases of lost children, lost parents, lost houses, following the sweep of armies through the land and the flight of refugees hither and thither, both in front of advancing troops, and in their wake. A case of the kind Mrs

Moorehead described was therefore not unusual, but by 1953 becoming rare.

'I think this seems to be a close family affair,' Mrs Moorehead persisted. 'There is a possibility that it may have concerned the business group of Luccini, the big travel agents. An accidental death, perhaps, involving the mother or wife of a director, a partner even.'

By this time the head of the Press library was called, since the junior who was serving Mrs Moorehead felt quite out of his depth. The chief librarian asked a few questions, stared, but ordered certain old volumes to be brought out. They were dated November and December of 1953.

'These may assist you, signora,' the librarian said and went away.

There were various obituaries, including two in the Luccini name, one for Paula, wife of Federico, tragically drowned, together with her infant son, Filippo. In later editions there were notices of the accident concerned, of suspected suicide, of the failure to find the body of the child.

This seemed to be exactly what Mrs Moorehead and Carlotta were looking for. They made a note of the dates concerned, of the name of the paper that had published the news, together with the name of the editor at the time. Then they went back to their hotel to consult Mr Moorehead about their next move.

He decided to make it in person. He had business connections in Italy, spoke the language fluently, with barely a trace of English accent, and had little difficulty in arranging an interview with one of the Luccini directors, a grandson of the founder of the firm, a stoutish, but alert-looking man in his forties.

When Mr Moorehead was announced to him in his office he said, 'You are the second enquirer to come to us, asking for details of that tragedy.'

'The first being your police, on behalf of Interpol?' asked Mr Moorehead smiling.

'Correct. I see now that the matter is more serious than I expected. I was inclined to resent it as an impertinence.'

'Because it brought up again a sorrow long forgotten with the passage of time?'

'Never forgotten! It was an unforgivable act!'

'We are speaking of Signora Luccini's death? That was unforgivable? May I ask why? I mean in no way an insult by asking.'

After a sultry pause, while Luccini's face grew deep red in colour, he said, with obvious reluctance, 'My Aunt Paula committed suicide, signor. She left a message, a note, giving her intention.'

'But the child?'

'Ah, the child!' Luccini banged a fist on

233

his desk. 'To kill herself, a mortal sin, without cause of any kind, for a mad reason, that was unforgivable! To take the boy with her, an act of true insanity!'

'The child's body was never found, I believe,' Mr Moorehead ventured cautiously.

'Never. But one could not expect it. She was found in the sea below the cliffs near Sorrento. Over a week after she disappeared.'

'Which was when, exactly?'

The date was just what he expected: there seemed to be no point in any further question. The father was called Federico. The name was vaguely familiar to Mr Moorehead, but he could not at that moment recall why.

Which prompted, nevertheless, one last question.

'The father–' he began.

Again Luccini brought his fist down on his desk top.

'My uncle? Devastated. Out of his mind. Murderous. For weeks, searching secretly, he did not care for publicity, with his name, of course. But never any clues. Or none that we, his relations, ever heard of. But we did hear him swear, several times over the years, that if anyone knew what had prompted that suicide or brought it about, he would kill that person. I am sure he meant it.'

'Did the note, then, suggest she might

have been guided, or persuaded, towards suicide?'

Mr Luccini drew himself up: the interview was at an end. Mr Moorehead saw that he had gone a little too far. He rose himself and held out his hand.

'I must not trespass on your valuable time any longer,' he said in a formal business voice. 'I thank you very much for your indulgence over this painful matter. In a way it concerns my own family, as I hope in due course to be able to explain to you.'

They parted, politely, the last question unanswered.

'If I had insisted, I thought I might get a knife in my guts or a shot in my head,' Mr Moorehead said to his wife and daughter when he described this meeting. 'Quite frightening. Fat little bloke, but *fierce!* Anyway, I think we are home and dry as far as Phil is concerned. He looks very much like being a Luccini, doesn't he? Better leave it to Interpol to clear up the detail, hadn't we?'

'Can't we tell Phil? I can't keep it in much longer?' Carlotta said, her excitement and relief very plain, her colour high, her eyes brilliant.

'Tell you what, darling,' her father, besottedly admiring, told her. 'We'll tell him to join us in Milan and that the news is good, so far.'

235

'Why Milan?'

'Because they're doing *Figaro* just now, and I want real opera for a change. Italian production. Mostly Italian singers, Italian audience.'

So they agreed to that.

Philip took the invitation to join the Mooreheads in Milan as an indication that they had real news for him. He accepted with a long-distance telephone call to their hotel. He still had a self-earned balance at his bank and had in no way begun to understand what poverty meant, in real, relative or assumed trade union terms. So the habits and conveniences of moderate wealth he took for granted, as he had done all his life.

If he wondered at Milan as the meeting place rather than a more attractive one on the shores of Lake Lugano, the reason for it was soon explained. They had stopped at Milan on their way north to see and hear *Figaro,* since Mozart was the parents' favourite composer, in all of his marvellous range. The children, Carlotta, her sisters and young brother, were all musical, the boy sang.

Carlotta explained that she shared this view of classical music, but found modern serious jazz more rewarding. Philip confessed to overall ignorance of both kinds of music, but a willingness to sample each.

The posters in the streets showed advertisements of the current opera season and of other entertainments. These included theatre plays, films, sporting events and in huge, coloured pictures of spangled men and women, horses, dogs, elephants, sealions, comedians and acrobats, one of the most celebrated of European travelling circuses, featuring its most distinguished performer, the great Federico Luccini.

The name hit Mr Moorehead with blinding force. Of course, Federico. Marvellous high-wire stuff. He'd seen him in Germany, twice when he was in Cologne on business. And in Strasbourg on a French trip. Federico Luccini, Philip Bennet's real father, beyond doubt.

'But we can't, we mustn't, tell him yet,' Mrs Moorehead pleaded when she was alone with her husband that night.

'No. I see that,' he answered. 'I must say I jolly well nearly did out with it when we saw the poster of the circus. Carlotta would never have kept it in if I hadn't managed to push on quickly before she could take it in.'

'Thank heaven you wouldn't tell the children the full story of your interview with the Luccini chairman in Naples.'

'Too right.'

So, at Philip's eager insistence, the party of seven, on the day following their visit to the opera-house, went to the Milan equivalent of a British big top and sat in the second row near the centre where the horses' hooves spattered them occasionally with the soft covering of the ring and the exciting smells of scent and grease-paint, sweat, hide, and animal dung, vied with those of a huge, enthusiastic audience.

It was an unusually hot evening, after an overpoweringly hot day. The men were all in their shirt sleeves, though Mr Moorehead carried a linen jacket over his arm. Philip had brought a summer linen suit with him, though he had left a wet, cold, August day at Heathrow two days before. He also had shorts for the Lakes, but wore the linen trousers with a thin sweat-shirt this evening, out of courtesy to Mrs Moorehead.

He was excited by the whole lay-out of his surroundings at the circus. This was something his mother had never taken him to see as a child. He had never bothered to take himself to one in England when he grew up.

But now he knew he had missed something, perhaps that thing he was now enjoying at his advanced school of gymnastics in England.

The prime turn of the evening began. The high-wire act. After the great trapezes had swung to and fro, picking up performers in mid-air, dropping them, transferring them by hands, by feet, dangling them by knees, by teeth even, depositing them and their astonishing men and girls on the platforms, high above the ground, there was a hush.

Then the wire appeared, stretched from side to side, sixty feet or more from the ground, shining in the spotlights. The band began its low drum-roll and from the left-hand upper platform stepped the Great Federico with his pole, a trim spangled figure like the rest, dark hair covering a head held high and facing forward to the platform opposite, unsupported by any other act or any other artiste, no net below to catch him if the wire broke, or–

He went through movements and antics of such dexterity and amazing balance that Philip gasped in astonished delight and awe.

Then at about the middle of the wire the unheard-of happened. The pole broke in two between the performer's hands. The pieces fell away on either side. The drum-roll increased to cover the short cries from the man on the wire, cries of command, not of fear, but cries that sent half a dozen attendants running. The band stopped abruptly.

While a gasp of horrified astonishment from the audience was followed by shouts and screams, the ringmaster ran to the middle of the floor, imploring everyone to keep their seats, to be quiet and helpful, to assist the rescue, which in his heart he believed to be impossible.

'For he has not fallen!' the ringmaster kept repeating. 'You see, he has not fallen!'

And indeed, he had not. The Great Federico had dropped his useless pole fragments and allowing himself to stoop swiftly, had seized the wire itself first with one hand, then the other and swung clear of it. The audience, still terrified, clapped wildly, the band, totally unhinged, began a subdued drum-roll all over again in an agony of indecision.

But Philip, who understood the implications, had already acted. He knew what the broken pole implied. He had broken one himself at an early attempt and had fallen ten feet. He had studied this act: he had already practised a few variations, without a pole.

His action took even the ringmaster by surprise. At the foot of the left-hand ladder Philip demanded a harness. His Italian was still lamentable, but in the trade they were used to all tongues and some knew enough English to help.

Yes, they had a harness, up on the platform, but Federico had always refused to wear it. Always. Now it was denied him, there was no one to take it to him, without falling himself.

'I will take it, on myself,' Philip promised. 'And bring him down with me.'

He spoke so surely, with such confidence,

such energy, that those at the foot of the ladder gave way and Philip ran up it to the platform.

Here he met with less resistance. Those who had the harness and understood how to manage its use in supporting, raising or lowering the wearer, were only too pleased to fix him into it, while one of them called to the dangling acrobat to tell him what was proposed.

Federico nodded. If he had to die, well he would not be too proud to allow this attempt, though he thought it must fail, and in so doing shake him from the wire into that fall for which he had been prepared, without regrets, ever since he had lost his son, his hoped-for successor, Filippo.

In the audience the Mooreheads clung to one another. Carlotta was moaning, 'He'll fall! It's crazy! Crazy!' Her father held her close, with an arm round her shoulders.

They had switched the lights to the platform. Federico could see that his would-be rescuer was a young foreigner, not one of his own people, and that he was, indeed, protected by a harness. So he would not, himself, be the cause of another's death.

He held on: he was not weakening yet: it would be a straightforward question of timing.

And so it was. Philip refused the pole. He kicked off his canvas shoes. He rolled his trousers up to the knee, he waited until the light swung round to show him very clearly the narrow path before him and the two hands of the Great Federico clasping the wire. He stepped out from the platform.

The band stopped. The audience held its breath. One or two parents clapped hands over their children's mouths.

Philip, unhesitating, moved steadily forward. He stopped, left foot forward, and crouched, knees well apart, as he had been taught. Now was the moment. He must reach down, secure the man before he himself overbalanced. It was a matter of seconds, of timing.

Federico did the timing. He stared up at his rescuer. He said in a sharp staccato Italian, 'The right hand, at three. One, two, THREE!'

He took his own left hand from the wire as Philip's right shot out to meet it. They locked above the wrist and still Philip balanced on the wire, fortified by feeling the harness tighten about him.

'The left! One, two, THREE!'

They were joined, they left the wire. Philip, with extended arms, head first, trying to get his legs together and straight behind him. The band burst out into the usual triumph at the successful finish of an act and kept it up until the two men landed neatly, separated and bowed.

Then the applause rang out in clapping, in shouts and cries of 'Bravo! Bravissimo!' repeated in waves of joy and relief. It seemed it would never stop.

All those in the ring waved their arms and bowed, over and over again. They surrounded the two, they unfastened Philip from the harness, they brought his canvas shoes, they pulled down his linen slacks, a girl in a frilly tou-tou ran up with sheaves of congratulatory flowers. The Mooreheads clapped and shouted with the rest. Carlotta wept freely and unashamed.

But Philip and Federico stared and stared at one another, unheeding the audience, the noise, the excited crowd of their colleagues milling round them. Philip saw a man of about his own height, with the broad shoulders and narrow hips of an athlete, all muscle in leg and arm: muscles of steel that he had felt with awe in that mad swoop from near ceiling to welcome ring floor. The head, below him as they went down, was bald in the middle, the eyes, so near him now, were as black as his own, but with the white ring of age already visible about the pupil. Federico saw the face, the well-remembered face, of his own youth; his own face at thirty, smooth, close-shaven, curly black hair, longer than he had ever worn, with small black side-burns. But still his own face.

Philip said, in halting Italian, 'I think you must be my father.'

Federico said, in an awed voice, 'It is a miracle! It is a dream I lost. A son to follow me! You *are* my son!' He took his hand from Philip's wrist where it had lain since they had faced the audience, bowing again and again. He put his arms round his rescuer and kissed him on both cheeks.

Renewed shouts, laughter and clapping made them turn. Walking towards them across the ring, escorted by the ringmaster, were Detective Superintendent Holmes in a dark suit and an officer of the Italian branch of Interpol, in uniform.

17

Detective Superintendent Holmes, back in England, was less than satisfied with the result of his trip abroad. Way-out drama in an Italian circus was all very well in its way, but it afforded absolutely no help whatever in his standing problem, the murder of Mrs Bennet.

For though the mystery of Philip's parentage was solved with resulting exuberant joy throughout the Luccini empire of business interests and activities, that astonishing solution destroyed entirely any convenient revenge motive for the killing. The great acrobat Federico had raged and threatened for months after his wife's suicide. He had been at the height of his powers at the time: ever after, the family said, he had performed as if in a trance: the heart had gone out of him.

But he had not retired, never thought of it, the circus would have collapsed without his name on the billboards. And the full list of his activities, the dates and places, over the years, were all recorded. There had been no visits to England. As in the case of the superlative Swiss clown, Grock, London was banned by the English tax laws. At no time whatever, and definitely not within the last six months, had Federico been in England. In 1953 he had performed with the circus in Germany and Austria. His wife had been left with their long-hoped-for son. She was known to have acted strangely. In the suicide letter she had expressed her fears for the child, for she knew his father would want to train him in his own art from the earliest possible moment. So, it was concluded, she had taken the infant with her in her plunge from the cliffs. The poor mite had died from falling, without knowing his fate, while her obsession was the fear that he would fall from the wire.

But now they knew that they had mistaken her message. Safe from the dangers of the circus, yes. A prosperous English upbringing. Safe indeed, except for his own inherited nature, inherited skills.

Back at the Broxbourne Incident Centre Holmes found the village seething with excitement. The fantastic story of their young Mr Bennet, their Phil or even Pip, as most of them called him, was the main topic of most conversations. He was the hero of a genuine exploit as well as the centre of a most intriguing tale of deception, fraud, child exploitation. And all shown up; finding, too, a happy ending, like the nicest kind of old-fashioned fairy tale. All the same, Holmes was right back where he started.

Or was he? Surely not, he decided. That business of the bones in that tin box had put him right off his main search. Well, not entirely, since it showed up Mrs Bennet in a true light. An unscrupulous woman in the grand manner, so probably in small things as well. Inconsiderate to the point of criminal outrage in playing upon the fears of that half-crazy Italian woman. Must have given her money for the child, the Luccinis thought. So why not some other less than honest act, at the expense of a character equally flawed?

Pullen. Joe Pullen. Another known seedy type, who had not fully accounted for himself on the night he had visited Garwood House. The last night he went there on his blackmailing occasions. The night Mrs Bennet died.

Holmes sent for Detective Sergeant Miles. There was a full and useful report from that young man. It linked with Joe Pullen's scanty, reluctant information.

Miles had been delighted with the Italian scoop in the local paper, for he had supplied the tear-jerking episode in the old Weymouth commercial hotel. He had managed to locate the chambermaid, now a cheerful housewife and mother of four, who had looked after the young Bennet boy while his mother fetched her car. Little did she know, etcetera, and Detective Sergeant Miles, keenly searching for the truth, 'with that human touch of the British policeman–'

'You can get that human touch to work again, Tom,' said Detective Superintendent Holmes, 'taking very human precautions, of course, on that old villain, Pullen.'

'Follow him, sir?'

'Fill up at the garage and take note of the younger lads there. Find which car he uses, check the petrol consumption. We'll get the patrols on it, too. Find out if he had any sort of pattern of business visits. Bert Elbury at the pub here seems to think he had.'

'May I ask what this is in aid of, sir?'

'I want something up to date to hold over him while I ask him what really happened at Garwood on the night Mrs Bennet got the chop.'

Between them the two detectives managed an encounter that provided Holmes with the material he sought. Joe Pullen, stopping at the pub in Broxbourne, was greeted as usual by Elbury. He ordered his accustomed pint with a hot sausage roll and a helping of cheese and took it to the table where he had parked his briefcase. He was joined a few seconds later by Detective Superintendent Holmes, similarly provided with food and drink.

'Morning, Joe,' said Holmes. 'Don't interrupt your lunch. I'm having mine, too, you see?'

'Like hell you are! What is it now, for Christ sake?'

'Just a short chat about old times. Not here, perhaps.'

'You can't–'

'I've a car outside. Couple of lads in it. Won't keep you long. Don't hurry, though. All the time in the world.'

They ate in silence. It took about ten minutes. As they walked out together, Pullen first, two silent interchanges took place. A couple near the door half rose as the garage owner reached them. He waved a hand to and fro in front of him. As Holmes passed the bar he looked at Bert Elbury behind it. The landlord nodded.

At the Broxbourne Incident Centre Pullen refused a cigarette, but lit one of his own small, thin cheroots. He blew smoke across the table at Holmes and asked defiantly, 'So what?'

'I think you know,' Holmes told him. 'I have now checked with Elbury at the pub that you are the man who drove in just on closing time, looking whitish-green and shaking all over. He thought you were going to be sick and in fact you went straight to the toilet and were.'

'So what?' asked Pullen again.

'So the next day when the news of the murder broke in the village, Bert wondered. But he didn't want to be mixed up in anything, so he didn't come forward. Later, when we seemed flummoxed, which we were, he was afraid to say it all, just that he'd had a late caller who wasn't very well, but wasn't drunk and drove away after having a drink.'

'Brandy and water. I felt God-awful.'

'Better tell me now, Joe. The old story is all known. You blackmailed her on a suspicion that was a smart guess, didn't you? She refused to pay that last time. You lost your cool and hit her and–'

'Balls!' shouted Pullen in a high voice. 'Bloody balls! She was dead! Never refused me, never would have done!'

Holmes looked at him with steady eyes, then said, 'Suppose you tell me what happened that night. The full story. The true one. After you left your car in the lane, in the usual place.'

'Which I didn't.'

'Oh, why not?'

'Because the place was taken already. It was the obvious point to pull in off the road, near the main entrance. The big old gates were never locked, hardly ever shut, in Mrs Bennet's time.'

'So what did you do?'

'Drove up to the house for once. It never really mattered, only as the boy grew up I thought he might get nosey, his mum seeing men late at night. But I knew he was away at that school he taught at.'

'Go on.'

'I got out and rang the bell. No answer. I tried several times, then I walked round the house. There were lights in the lounge, where she always saw me. She'd said she'd be there when I rang up earlier that day for interview. Never tried to put me off. Knew I meant what I said when I told her I'd turn her in if she didn't.'

'Bastard!' Holmes murmured, but Pullen only grinned at this lapse of police manners.

'Go on,' said the detective again, roughly.

'The garden window door was closed, but not locked. The curtain was drawn. I went in and there she was, on the floor, near her usual chair, with her head smashed in. Quite dead, but warm. I felt her ankle, not her wrist. Both hands were near the head, as if she'd tried to protect it and both hands were bloody. I hadn't stepped more than a foot into the room. It was summer, well, just after the real season—'

'I know what the weather's been like this year,' Holmes told him, 'you needn't remind me.'

'I mean I was in thin clothes and canvas shoes. I wasn't leaving footprints. Nor the car any tyre marks, either.'

'Did you see any weapon, or anything that might be called a weapon?'

'No. I didn't wait. Not my business. Got

out quick, and drove off to the pub, feeling awful.'

'We know all about that. About the other car, the one in your usual parking place?'

'Still there. That made me feel worse as I passed it. The murderer must have been still in the room or in the house or in the garden. Though I hadn't got anyone in my lights as I drove up to the house or away from it. Still, plenty of room to hide in all those bushes and trees.'

'Plenty,' said Holmes. 'Now, Pullen, as you will have realised, I have your statement taped. I'll have it on paper for you to sign and then Sergeant Miles here will take you back to your car at the pub. You can say what you like to your mates there, if they are still there. And at the garage, but I suggest the less you explain the better. I'm inclined to believe you, all things considered. You're not the type to kill. But you'll be asked to describe your finding Mrs Bennet dead, when we do catch up on the murderer and bring him to trial. Take Mr Pullen away, Tom.'

'The pub of course was shut when we got back there,' Miles reported later. 'He perked up again, no end, and of course his pals had left, but his car was waiting for him.'

'I think we'll all give Pullen's garage a miss for the present,' said Holmes, laughing.

'You bet, sir.'

Pullen's story was much as they had expected, but new in one important respect. Why was the waiting car still there when Pullen left? Because he had been only a few minutes going up to the house, making his gruesome discovery and driving away again? Because it belonged to some quite innocent stranger whose business in the vicinity had been in progress when Pullen arrived? Not a visitor to the house, but in the neighbourhood? Or did it belong to the murderer, still on the premises? To an innocent stranger, could it be, with the murderer *belonging* to the premises?

A new thought this and a terrible one. Only Mrs Harper lived in. Surely not that family treasure, that standby, that elderly white-haired, nervous, loving housekeeper they all called Harpie?

'There's that couple in the flat over the garage,' suggested Miles. 'I know we went into their movements in great detail at the very start, but you do get surprises, don't you, sir? And foreigners, after all.'

'I agree,' said Holmes. 'No good leaning over backwards to pretend foreigners are just the same as us. We all know they aren't.'

'Some more than others,' said Tom, apologising for his extreme opinion in some cases.

'That's enough of that,' said his superior.

253

The word went forth, summoning to Garwood both Miss Tupper and Philip Luccini, who had come back to England to rearrange his affairs, after the Italian authorities had dealt with their end of the business.

He was glad to escape for a time. The family welcome in Naples had been overwhelming. His father, dangerously overexcited, had been forced into a nursing home, for at least a couple of weeks, the family physician said. The Moorehead family had followed their original plan to tour the Lakes. Even Carlotta submitted. She was at heart a very sensible girl.

Detective Superintendent Holmes explained the new evidence and its implications. Also why they had been asked so urgently to come back to Garwood.

'I have not explained the new situation to Mrs Harper,' Holmes told them. 'Because in the light of what I have said, I could hardly do so.'

'You don't suspect *Harpie?*' they both cried.

'No. Not really. But she is very easily upset—'

'And you think she might let it all out to the real culprit?'

'Possibly. With disastrous results, not only for herself.'

'Oh!'

They knew why they were there. To give a complete list of the dailies who had worked at Garwood all those years, regardless of whether or not they had any kind of grudge against Mrs Bennet. For after all, Holmes explained, the case might be the frequent kind; of burglary with violence. There were valuable things in the house. Pure ordinary greed, encouraged perhaps by an aggressive boy-friend.

'Well,' said Aunt Amy, 'I don't know so much about dailies. Why not include all the staff living in, both at the time of Florence's marriage and after it.'

Holmes looked surprised, then annoyed.

'Were there any?' he asked. 'Hadn't the rot, as you'd call it, set in by then? Must I include Mr Grant, the chauffeur, as well as the Savins?'

'Most certainly not,' Philip said. 'Though he did stay on for a time because I remember him showing me the engine of the car and I must have been about three, I suppose.'

'More likely two or less,' said Aunt Amy. 'You always wanted to see the insides of machines, from the time you could toddle. And I don't see Mrs Somerton staggering back up the drive, even if she did get someone to drive her to the main gates.'

Both she and Philip found it hard to recall

those dailies until they were allowed to call in Mrs Harper to help, much against the detective's better judgement.

'She's the only person who might remember,' Philip insisted. 'After all, she usually found the new ones for my non-mother, even if she didn't actually engage them.'

Mrs Harper, a sadly crushed, bewildered-looking shadow of herself, submitted to the police officer's questions. She began a list of recent additions, then said, 'Some of them have given extra help at short notice off and on for years. I'm thinking of Mandy Williams. She's the younger sister of Gladys, who was here, living in, I believe, to help Mrs Bennet with – only it wasn't–!'

Here Mrs Harper broke down, and hid her face in her hands.

Philip sprang up to put his arms round her and comfort her, kneeling beside her and murmuring that he was still Pip, her Pip and always would be.

But Miss Tupper, who had also risen in her excitement, said, 'Gladys! Of course, Gladys! Percy dismissed her at once when he found she had left Florence alone that night. Gladys was devoted to Pip; he might have been her own. She'd even saved up to get him that toy he could never be parted from–'

She stopped suddenly: she collapsed into her chair again: she gave a weak, small cry of distress, fumbling for a handkerchief, shaking her head from side to side.

Detective Superintendent Holmes stared at his assembled helpers in amazement and a kind of horror. He felt he was in danger of immediate drowning in this sudden tidal wave of emotion that had poured into the room. But he took a grip on himself: he was his usual calm, not over-quick, but altogether dependable self when Miss Tupper managed to say, brokenly, 'Oh, what a fool I've been! Not to notice! Not to remember!'

'Miss Tupper, *please!* What have you just remembered?'

With Mrs Harper and Philip, faces lifted towards her; with Holmes and Miles eagerly alert to hear, Aunt Amy explained that vital lead to the true end of their search.

18

It took place, inevitably, to begin with, at Mrs Somerton's small house in Broxbourne. And only just in time.

The old woman had been afflicted for more than a week by one of those feverish colds that the general public call 'summer 'flu'. Her doctor knew that it was another bout of her chronic bronchitis, from which she had suffered for many years, regardless of the season or the weather.

This was the second expedition the two detectives, together with Philip and Aunt Amy, had made that afternoon, following Miss Tupper's enlightenment. The first visit had been to Mandy Williams. She was quite willing to talk about her sister.

'Poor old Glad,' she said. 'A year older than me, but always the shy one of the family. The boys never took much notice of her, though she aimed to get married and have a family. It upset her when they came to take me out and not one ever came for her. They found her too awkward, I suppose.'

'But she had this job with Mrs Bennet?'

'Oh yes. Very proud of herself. The poor

lady hadn't a clue how to manage the baby. Depended on her entirely, she always said.'

'And gave him the bone teething ring?' This was Philip.

'Yes.'

'Describe it,' Detective Superintendent Holmes ordered.

'Well, not real bone, but sort of cream-coloured. Three little bells that made a pretty noise when you shook it.'

'I told you,' Miss Tupper broke in. 'Three! When it was dug up, *two* only. And I forgot! Must be getting senile!'

'You are sure there were three?' Holmes insisted.

'Oh yes. You see Gladys made no end of fuss when Mrs Bennet and the baby–' She broke off, looking embarrassed.

'Never mind what we all know now,' Holmes urged. 'Tell us what Gladys did when Mrs Bennet came back.'

'Well, she'd expected to be re-engaged. But Mrs Bennet had a trained nursery nurse at Garwood in a matter of hours. So Glad was heart-broken.'

'And then?'

'She didn't know Mrs Harper, of course, so she didn't like to call. But she was working locally, still, so she managed when they were out, Mrs Bennet and Mrs Harper both, and got herself known to Mrs Savin, who was sorry for her when she heard the tale of Glad being fired and that. Let her go up to the nursery. After that – it was after that – she began to talk of the baby not being the same one, not the real little Master Pip.'

Holmes nodded.

'So we concluded she found the missing bell off the ring and jumped to that far-fetched conclusion.'

Mandy was annoyed.

'Don't look at me as if I'd stolen something. I thought she was round the bend and told her so. She did have a couple of months' treatment for what they called depression.'

'Where was that?'

Mandy named a geriatric and psychiatric clinic attached to the cottage hospital, both now swept away in the general centralising of the Health Service. Holmes made a note of it, but felt this was of doubtful value. However, her local G.P. might have notes: it could wait.

'And later she found work? Always has had jobs?'

Miss Tupper intervened.

'She had, indeed. In business, isn't it, Mandy? I may say I made it my concern to ask about her and follow her progress, because Florence always seemed unwilling to do so; never wanted to see her, and then seemed to forget her entirely. So I took over the interest for a time. She did very well.'

'She got her own shop,' Mandy declared with pride. 'Baby outfitting, clothes and all that, up to five years old. In Dorchester.'

She gave Holmes the address. Philip said, 'I don't think I ever saw her, did I? Does she come often to see you, Mandy?'

'Not often. Not once all this summer. Until today.'

Startled, angry, Detective Superintendent Holmes leaped to his feet. *Today! Here!*

Mandy stared at him. Why all this, now? She answered slowly, mildly, as usual.

'Why not? Yes, she was here up till an hour or so ago. Then she went off in her car. No, I don't know where, but most like to see old Somerton. She's been bad, I've heard, with this summer 'flu that's going about. What's the excitement in that, I should like to know?'

But she never got an answer, for Holmes with Detective Sergeant Miles and the two from Garwood House had disappeared and she heard their cars start up into violent action before she got to the door to see their sharp turn across the road.

There was a car parked beside Mrs Somerton's villa at the other, the new end of Broxbourne. Miles stopped beyond it and backed on to it, a few feet away from its front bumper. A patrol car, summoned by

262

Holmes as they shot through the village, came up behind to block it securely; Philip stopped behind the patrol car. The occupants of all three cars got out, but the patrol were told by Holmes to wait outside the house, unless called for. He and the others went on to the front door.

It was not locked. It opened at the turn of the handle and they all went in without knocking or ringing the bell. Holmes knew the way into Mrs Somerton's sitting room, but the old woman was not there. Miss Tupper pointed the way to her bedroom, also on the ground floor, where she had taken her bed of late, to avoid the stairs as she grew more infirm.

Holmes went on ahead, again without knocking. The others crowded after him.

Mrs Somerton was in bed. Gladys was beside the bed. Mrs Somerton's face was hidden because Gladys's hands had covered it with Mrs Somerton's pillow, which she was holding down firmly, while her right knee controlled the old woman's struggles, now grown weak as the smothering progressed to its intended end.

In a couple of bounds the two detectives reached the bedside and while Holmes seized Gladys, Tom snatched away the pillow and lifted up an apparently moribund Mrs Somerton.

When the tumult was over, the old woman,

sustained by artificial respiration until the ambulance came, and by oxygen until it reached the hospital, and Gladys, hand-cuffed to Miles, was taken to the Incident Centre, the final explanations were arrived at with less than complete satisfaction for Detective Superintendent Holmes.

Gladys was no longer reticent. On the contrary, she was inclined to boast. She laughed, very merrily, when Holmes asked her for an explanation of why she wanted to kill Mrs Somerton.

'The old bag threatened me,' she said. 'Told me the whole thing was wide open now. Mr Philip, as she called him, was back with his real family, Mrs Bennet was shown up, those Thorntons would get Garwood and nobody wanted to know who'd bumped off that wicked deceiver she'd hated from the day her own Percy married her.'

'Mrs Somerton was wrong,' Holmes told her. 'We wanted to know. We still do. I think it was you killed Mrs Bennet, Miss Doe.'

That silenced her. Holmes explained, as fully as he could, the grounds of his conclusion, pressing chiefly his belief that she was in the house when Joe Pullen had driven up and seen the dead body, the wound and the blood.

'Why wasn't it him that did it?' Gladys asked.

'He had no motive for murder. You, it

264

seems, had.'

Miss Tupper then explained about the teething ring and the missing bell.

'I think you found it, Gladys, when you managed, with Mrs Savin's help, to see the nursery. I think you found it, in that play cupboard perhaps.'

'No. Caught in a woolly vest I'd knitted him, at the back of the drawer I'd always used for his little undies, but she never did,' Gladys burst out. 'That made me wild, her not caring, not showing the new nurse where we put things. And Mrs Savin said he never had the ring to her knowledge, only some little flimsy wooden thing that he didn't much care for, got broken pretty soon. I spoke to the nurse once in the village. She knew nothing of any ring, neither. That I gave him, saved up for it, I did, and he never would be parted from it.'

It was an old tale, the old monotonous complaint. The listeners shrank away to hear it. Miss Tupper swallowed the next question she had been about to ask, but Holmes pressed on.

'So Mrs Somerton fed your jealousy and your sorrow at losing the care of the child. It all boiled up again when he came into the estate. It drove you to decide to get rid of Mrs Bennet, didn't it?'

'Not her. She was all for that good-for-nothing Reg of hers. I didn't care tuppence

265

for him. No, it was that other one, that ought to have been at Garwood all along.'

'Do you mean Mrs Thornton?'

'Not her. Treat you like mud. Worse than old Percy himself. The young one. Tig. Smashing, in a way. Not that I didn't see through him, the young liar.' She laughed again, more chillingly this time than before.

'Are you telling me that Tig Thornton incited you to murder?' Holmes asked.

'He buttered me up and told me she'd be better out of the way and then he and his father could dispute who this Mr Bennet really was.'

Philip murmured to Aunt Amy, 'She's mad, poor thing. Stark staring bonkers.'

Gladys heard him. It drove her over the border. She screamed out, 'It was justice! She had to go! She killed my baby, mine! She broke his toy! Murderess! Cheat! Thief! Yes, I found the bell, Mrs Somerton knows I found it. Tig knows I found it. Tig will have Garwood, he promised me, silly boy, liar too—'

She was standing up, stamping her feet to drive her words into her audience's minds, into their hearts. They were staring at her with stony, hostile eyes, as most people always had regarded her. She suddenly gave up, feeling for her chair, which Miles held and into which he lowered her exhausted form.

A policewoman appeared, summoned to the Incident Centre from Mrs Somerton's house. Tea appeared, distributed to all present. And still Detective Superintendent Holmes waited, determined to clinch his case, though he began to fear there could be no conviction, since the killer would be found unfit to plead.

When calm was fully restored and both Philip and Aunt Amy showed definite signs of rebellion at any longer delay, Holmes began again in a very reasonable friendly voice.

'So, Gladys, you considered it your duty to do away with Mrs Bennet? When did you finally decide that?'

'Not to kill, just to show her up. Make her tell.'

'So you went to the house one night? You have a car. Did you use it?'

'Yes. Left it outside the gates like I'd seen others do when I was living there.'

'Did Mrs Bennet answer the bell, or was it Mrs Harper?'

'Neither of them. It was lateish, nearly eleven, but only just dark. I went to the long windows and knocked. She pulled back the curtains and let me in. The lights were on. She didn't properly see it was me at first. When she did she told me to go away, said she was expecting a visitor.'

'Did she say who it was?'

'Not she. I guessed it was a man, though, and I was right.'

'So you did not go. You accused her of killing your baby.'

Gladys sprang up again.

'I never! I didn't waste my breath! I saw those flowers in the big bowl in the hearth, as she always had them in summer time. I saw the fire-irons, showing beside and behind them. I took the big tongs by the handle and brought them down on her head and she fell on her face and she didn't move, not once, she didn't.'

Tongs? Fire-irons? Holmes thought furiously, but to no effect. They had checked everything, but *everything!* So how had they missed out on the tongs? He looked across at Miles.

'Every possible weapon in the hearth, sir,' that young man declared, with emphasis.

Again Gladys laughed and went on laughing.

'No blame to you, Mr Holmes,' she spluttered, 'because I wasn't so silly as to leave it with her. Oh no! I knew my way about that house. I just wrapped my handkerchief round the tongs and took them away to the pantry and gave them and my hands and the hankie a good wash and then a polish wearing the rubber gloves we always kept with the cleaning things. The front door bell rang twice while I was at it, but I paid no attention, only waited a good long time before I went back to the drawing room as she called it, to put the tongs back. Then I put the rubber gloves back in the pantry and left the way I'd come in. Rubbing off the door handles, of course.'

'Of course,' said Holmes. 'Your prints and Pullen's.'

'Pardon?'

'Never mind.'

He did not mind. He had it all now and though he charged Gladys Doe with the murder of Mrs Bennet and the attempted murder of Mrs Somerton, he decided that he was well rid of one of the most unsatisfactory cases he had ever had to handle.

But Miss Tupper and Philip left the Incident Centre feeling too shattered to talk to one another, wishing only to get away alone and grieve in solitude over the wrongs and cruelties quite ordinary-seeming people inflicted upon each other in their greed and self-centred loves and fears.

But as he turned his car into the drive of Garwood House Philip said, 'I must tell Harpie everything. The real truth of it all. From the beginning. Harpie has been my real mother all the time, not those other two, the grabber and the suicide. I can't bear to stay in this place a day longer than I must. The Luccinis have promised to set me up any way I want. Well, Carlotta says she'll marry me, my father says I must have a job in the circus–'

'But not on the wire!' cried Miss Tupper.

'Definitely not. What I mean is, Harpie must go with me and the Savins too, if they'll come. Can you think of a vacant house with garden anywhere in your direction, Aunt Amy?'

'I'll do my best,' she said.

And so she did, with success, quite soon.

The publishers hope that this book has given you enjoyable reading. Large Print Books are especially designed to be as easy to see and hold as possible. If you wish a complete list of our books please ask at your local library or write directly to:

Dales Large Print Books
Magna House, Long Preston,
Skipton, North Yorkshire.
BD23 4ND

This Large Print Book, for people
who cannot read normal print,
is published under the auspices of

THE ULVERSCROFT FOUNDATION